Dear Romance Reader,

Welcome to a world of breathtaking passion and never-ending romance.
Welcome to *Precious Gem Romances*.

It is our pleasure to present *Precious Gem Romances*, a wonderful new line of romance books by some of America's best-loved authors. Let these thrilling historical and contemporary romances sweep you away to far-off times and places in stories that will dazzle your senses and melt your heart.

Sparkling with joy, laughter, and love, each *Precious Gem Romance* glows with all the passion and excitement you expect from the very best in romance. Offered at a great affordable price, these books are an irresistible value—and an essential addition to your romance collection. Tender love stories you will want to read again and again, *Precious Gem Romances* are books you will treasure forever.

Look for fabulous new *Precious Gem Romances* each month—available only at Wal★Mart.

Kate Duffy
Editorial Director

MY FAVORITE FLAVOR

Deborah Shelley

Zebra Books
Kensington Publishing Corp.

http://www.zebrabooks.com

To everyone who has helped proofread, critique, and brain-storm this book—Carol Webb, David Mosley, Jessica Mosley, Kimi Watters, Marion Ekholm, Nancy Neal, Pam Wertz, and Sandra Lagesse. You guys are the best!

And to Nan Robinson, our inspiration.

Chapter One

Tess Samuels was sure there were worse things than having her body fat measured in public, but right now, she couldn't think of a single one. However, as the medical technician yelled her weight across the table to the person who performed the function of recording every embarrassing detail with what appeared to be great relish, Tess realized that nothing could be this bad.

Thoughts of throttling the cute, petite technician and her enthusiastic assistant right there in the staff cafeteria danced through Tess's head. She'd never forgive the new management of Amanda Rae Ice Cream for forcing everyone here at their Washington, D.C. headquarters to go through this mandatory health screening. And right after the Christmas holidays, too. Maybe she'd throttle the whole executive team, while she was at it.

"We're done here." The technician took the piece

of paper from her helper. She looked at Tess, shook her head, and sighed. "You weigh more than I thought."

Tess felt the heat rush to her cheeks. How could she let this dig go by without a snappy remark? She racked her brain for just the right comeback. "Oh, really?" Not even remotely snappy, but who could think straight when everyone in the whole room was staring at her in horror?

"Yes, really." Apparently, the technician didn't notice Tess's attempt at wit. "You need to take this form over to the next station. They'll be doing your cholesterol test and the rest of your blood work." She pointed.

Form in hand, Tess followed the rubbing alcohol fumes across the company cafeteria, averting her head as she passed some of the other research and development staff standing in line, waiting their turn for public humiliation.

Tess's best friend, Lorraine Johnson, an elegantly tall woman with flawless brown skin, was just leaving the blood drawing station. She put her hand on Tess's shoulder. "It's not that bad, girlfriend. If you survive, I'll meet you upstairs in my office for a chocolate fix."

As if Lorraine, with her long, slender build, had anything to worry about. Lorraine could eat anything—twice—and still not gain an ounce. But this was, as far as Tess was concerned, one of her friend's few faults.

Tess nodded at Lorraine and wordlessly handed the damning paper to a deceptively harmless-looking man wearing thick glasses. The thought occurred to her that he might not be able to find her arm, let alone her vein. She shrugged out of her suit jacket.

"Sit down and roll up your sleeve," he instructed, squinting as though he were having trouble seeing her at all.

With a deep sigh, Tess sat in the battered folding chair next to him, unbuttoned her cuff, and shoved her sleeve above her elbow. Squeezing her eyes tightly shut, she turned her head and held her breath.

The man twisted a latex strap tightly around her upper arm and started jabbing the area around her vein with his index finger.

"You know, if you shut your eyes, you really don't have to turn your head, too," someone near her whispered huskily.

Unconvinced, Tess kept her eyes closed and her head turned. She gasped as the strap was tightened even more.

"He hasn't even stuck the needle in yet." The observer chuckled softly.

Great. The man couldn't find her vein, and the needle was undoubtedly close to the size of the Washington Monument. And an overly interested bystander with a gravelly voice felt compelled to offer play-by-play commentary.

"Are we almost done here?" she choked out.

"Your veins are too small." She felt the technician pinch her arm. "And they roll," he complained, slapping her on the same spot with quick, stinging blows.

"Don't you have a smaller needle?" the unseen observer asked in a Rod Stewart kind of whisper. "There's no need for you to bruise her arm like that."

"Bruise?" Tess repeated in a small voice. Her palms began to sweat.

"Of course you're going to bruise," the technician said crossly, as if it were *her* fault. "You've got bad veins and you won't hold still. I've been doing this for twelve years, so I know what I'm doing. I had to stick the last person with veins like yours six or seven times before we got anything. In fact, we finally had to use his earlobe."

The biting coldness of rubbing alcohol made Tess feel faintly sick. She just knew she could hear the blood rushing from her head to her elbow, and with that thought, she began to sink into a well of blissful blackness. Her trip to oblivion came to a screeching halt, rudely interrupted by the stinging sensation of ammonia in her nasal passages.

As she jerked awake, she heard the snap of the latex strap being removed. Her vision cleared, and she found herself looking into a pair of magnificent gray eyes.

"Are you okay?"

She recognized the husky voice. So this was the man who'd tried to rescue her from the evil clutches of the licensed vampire.

"You fainted. I caught you before you hit the floor."

Which would explain the warm, muscular arm wrapped around her shoulders and the hand under her knees. She fought an overwhelming urge to snuggle closer. Tess noticed a small group of people gathered around them. Here she was with the man of her dreams . . . and an audience. Holding down the hem of her skirt with one hand, she struggled out of the stranger's hold. "I'm fine, really. Thank you."

"I'll get you something to drink." The gray-eyed man left and the crowd dispersed, leaving Tess alone with the technician.

He taped a cotton ball over what Tess knew had to be a crater-sized hole, and bent her elbow up. "Keep your arm in this position for a few minutes to stop the bleeding," he advised. "And put your head between your knees if you feel faint again. We don't want you passing out on us again, now do we?"

"No, we don't." Shakily, Tess straightened her arm, rolled down her sleeve, fastened her cuff, eased into her jacket, and walked carefully to the hallway. She still felt weak, but she couldn't stand everyone looking at her like that.

Waiting for the elevator, she gazed at herself in the polished brass doors. She didn't look like someone who had just faced death.

She turned, smoothing her bright red suit in the back. No way did she weigh as much as that broken scale had indicated. She was just . . . curvy. Swiveling, she tucked a stray tendril of her mahogany brown hair back into her chignon.

At the sound of someone behind her clearing his throat, she twirled around. Her tall, broad-shouldered rescuer had apparently witnessed every moment of her self-evaluation. No, Tess prayed—maybe he hadn't seen anything. Maybe he'd just gotten there.

He raised his eyebrow knowingly. "You forgot your juice," he rasped. He held out a paper cup.

Tess felt her face grow hot and knew for certain her pleas to heaven had been in vain. She turned quickly to face the elevator doors, hoping that he'd disappear. Or that she would.

"You still seem a little shaky. Why don't you come sit by me in the cafeteria until you're better?"

"No, thanks. I'm fine. Really. I just need to get to my office and—"

She literally leapt into the elevator as the doors opened. Horrified, she noticed that he followed right on her heels. Oh, great. Trapped with a handsome stranger. One who had not only seen her preening, something which she never did in public, but had also caught her when she fainted. He must think she was nuts.

"Here. You really should drink this." He held out the cup again, and this time she took it.

Tess could feel him studying her. It gave her goose-bumps. Glancing at him over the top of the cup, she noticed his magnificent, long, honey-blond hair. He looked as though he should be on the cover of some hot romance novel instead of standing next to her in the elevator of an ice cream manufacturing complex.

When they reached the tenth floor, the elevator stopped. He exited, then turned back toward the still open doors. "Red's always been my favorite color." He grinned, lifting that darned eyebrow again.

Which red? she wondered as the doors closed. Her red power suit . . . or her crimson cheeks? Oh well, obviously she didn't look as much like a cow as the little lady from hell had led her to believe. The scale really was broken. That was it.

Her knight in shining armor seemed to think she looked okay. And he sure smelled good. What was it? She closed her eyes and sniffed. Bread? Fresh-baked bread? She had to be losing it. It must be all that blood that had been so cruelly sucked from her veins.

Her elbow throbbed. Getting off the elevator, she headed straight for Lorraine's office. Tess grabbed a handful of M & Ms from the crystal bowl on the credenza.

Lorraine was nowhere in sight. She must have been called in to a last minute meeting. Taking a sticky note from a pad on her friend's desk, Tess wrote in her schoolteacher perfect script, *I survived. Barely. Give me a call when you get back.*

She took another handful of the chocolate candies, trying very hard to forget the rush of unfamiliar feelings the handsome stranger had aroused. It didn't work. Sighing, she went back to her own office and plopped down into her cushy leather chair. Thumbing idly through the monthly statistical report that had been delivered while she'd undergone torture in the staff cafeteria, she turned to the section on sales. She wondered what the public thought of their new Teddy Bear Fudge Brownie ice cream.

Evidently sales were through the roof. Tess smiled. When she first tasted her latest creation in the lab, she knew it would be a hit. Ten years in the business, and she was still on a roll. Not bad for a girl with a master's degree in Renaissance literature.

Wait until Lorraine saw these numbers, Tess thought. Forget the numbers. She wondered if Lorraine had seen the gray-eyed stranger. Grinning, she picked up the phone to see if her friend had gotten back to her office yet. Tess frowned as Lorraine's voice mail message came over the line. She was just about to say something when Lorraine plopped down on the edge of Tess's desk.

"You're still in one piece."

"I feel like I wrestled a porcupine. And lost." Tess grimaced. "That guy who drew everyone's blood was really creepy."

"Yeah. Rumor has it that you fell for him. Or on him." Lorraine winked. "Got any chocolate in here?"

"I always faint when I get the blood sucked out of my veins. I'm funny like that. And you know I always have chocolate here in the drawer."

Lorraine leaned over and started digging through the drawer next to her friend. "You're just about out. You've only got a couple of candy bars left."

"Help yourself. But I've only got one Baby Ruth left. And the day is still young."

Breaking the bar of chocolate into two pieces, Lorraine handed half to Tess. "Looks like you'll have to hit the vending machines."

"Yeah." Tess took the piece of candy and nibbled off a bite. "Did you see the guy in the booth next to the vampire table?"

"No."

"How did you miss him, Rainey? You're usually the first one to spot a Ten, and this guy was definitely an Eleven."

"I missed a Ten? But you never notice anyone. How did this one grab your attention?"

"He was hard to miss. I was in his arms."

"Fast work." Lorraine nodded approvingly. "Did you bother to introduce yourselves first?"

"I think he had laryngitis or something. He didn't

say much." Tess popped another piece of chocolate into her mouth.

"More action than words. Even better. So what happened? Were you so overcome by lust that you leaped into his arms?"

"I was so overcome by terror that I fainted into his arms."

Lorraine wadded up the empty wrapper and threw it at the wastebasket. "And here I thought you were the shy, quiet one. This is a side of you you've managed to keep hidden for the last ten years."

"I didn't plan it. It just happened." Tess opened the desk drawer and pulled out the last candy bar. "But you know what, Rainey?"

"What?" Lorraine held out her hand as Tess offered her half of the remaining Baby Ruth.

"I wish I'd gotten his name and phone number."

"You didn't get his name?" Lorraine shrieked. "I've failed in your training."

"But he knows where I work. If he's interested."

"He knows you work with eleven hundred other people here at Amanda Rae, and that's about it. How's he going to find you again? You should have given him a business card or something."

"I didn't think of it. Wouldn't you know it? My prince finally shows up, and I don't even have a glass slipper."

Chapter Two

It wasn't every day that a beautiful woman fell right into your arms. Zach Ferrara could just kick himself for not getting her name. And he'd had plenty of chances to ask her. He was out of practice. Way out of practice.

As soon as he'd finished writing up a complaint against the unprofessional technician who'd made her faint, he went back to the employee cafeteria to leave it with the company nurse. He spent a few minutes gathering up the leftover brochures he'd brought to the health fair from his own firm, Pure Heart Catering.

Zach looked around the room, hoping to see the lady in red again. He wondered how she was doing. He could still remember her scent. Chocolate. And cherry. Wow. Imagine a woman smelling like his favorite candy. Her scent could only be described as delicious.

It had felt so natural to have her in his arms. Of course, it would have been better if she'd been conscious.

Zach could visualize her reddish-brown hair loose and full and falling over her shoulders, not pulled back in that bun thing. He wondered how long her hair actually was.

He was sorry her skirt had gone all the way to her knees. Her calves were so shapely he'd liked to have seen another few inches of her legs. The memory of her knee against his hand made him want to run up and down every floor in the building until he found her again.

And the color of that suit. It was a serious red. A passionate red. A dangerous red. He wondered if the color was any indication of her personality. Hot and sensuous.

It was funny how priorities could change, Zach mused. When he'd gotten up this morning, his biggest problem had been the prospect of touting his catering company when he couldn't talk much. But losing his lady in red had made losing his voice pale in comparison.

He finished packing up his things and headed for his van.

Jalapeños and chocolate. Tess scratched her head with the end of her pencil and then crossed off the other ice cream creations on the list. Stretching, she slowly got up from her office chair and straightened her skirt. Running her finger along the bookshelves lining the wall, she drifted aimlessly to a window. The snow was beginning to fall, and through the twilight she could barely make out the Washington Monument.

Winters could be dreary in D.C., and something like a spicy chocolate creation might intrigue ice cream lovers. Chocolate Fiesta. Hot and sweet and chocolatey. This one had possibilities. It would probably sell well in the Southwest and might even tempt the tastebuds of the rest of the country. Southwestern flavors were popular right now.

Tess breathed on the windowpane and watched as it fogged over. She scribbled a picture of a jalapeño on top of an ice cream cone. If only she could overcome this uncharacteristic creative block she was experiencing, she might be able to get to the corner market for ingredients before the store closed for the evening. She sighed. It was no use. Her normally endless supply of ideas for ice cream flavors had dried up. Her brain was mush. And all because of him.

Never before had Tess been so distracted by any man, and certainly she'd never let one interfere with her work. Even the one guy she had dated for a short time in college had never affected her this way, and they'd seen each other every day. Now, here she was letting a man she'd only seen once, over a week ago, sabotage her creativity.

She turned from the window. Damn him, whoever he was. She couldn't let some stranger affect her this way. Grabbing her coat, she headed for the market. Maybe the smell of food would clear her head.

* * *

Zach knew he had to snap out of this . . . this . . . whatever it was. Even his loaves of bread weren't rising the way they should be. He'd burnt every batch of muffins for the last two weeks and his assistant, Nan, had taken to calling him a culinary disaster just waiting to happen. In fact, even his associate chefs barred him from their commercial oven.

And now, according to Nan, there was another Amanda Rae referral in their waiting area. Maybe this woman would be the one who had swooned so gracefully in his arms. Zach was tired of being disappointed. Dr. Andrews, the Amanda Rae company doctor, had referred a dozen different women to him as a result of the health screening, and not one of them had been his lady in red.

"Please send Ms. Logan in."

"Okay, boss." Nan wagged a finger at him. "But I have to warn you—she's not the one you're looking for. She's done her damnedest to become a blonde. But at least an inch of roots are screaming for bleach."

"Wouldn't you know it? It seems like half of Amanda Rae's employees are blondes. Natural or otherwise."

"Yeah, not everyone is lucky enough to be a brunette like me." Nan tossed her head. "I'm sure you wouldn't be looking for your mystery woman if she weren't a brunette. After all, everyone knows we're the best." Nan winked and sashayed to the door.

"Right." Zach laughed. He could always count on his sassy secretary to put him in a good mood. "We'll talk about that later, but right now, I have an appointment with Ms. Logan."

But Ms. Logan wasn't his lady in red. Neither was

Jane McCutcheon, Doree Taylor, Rachel Edelstein, and at least six other women. He wondered disconsolately if he'd ever see her again.

Two weeks after the mandatory health screening at Amanda Rae, Tess slumped down into the cushions of the company doctor's comfortable sofa, rereading the results of her evaluation. According to this, her body fat content was higher than that of her company's ice cream.

"Tess?"

Tess looked up. She'd been so appalled by what she was reading that she hadn't heard the doctor come into the room.

Dr. Andrews, a tall, big-boned woman with a gentle voice, sat down on an adjacent chair. "Have you finished reading that yet?" she asked. "We need to talk."

"It doesn't look too good, does it?" Tess began peeling the deep scarlet polish off her thumbnail.

Dr. Andrews shrugged. "I'd say that your cholesterol level has one foot in the danger zone and the other on a banana peel. And your blood pressure is on the high side."

"So, am I going to die?" Tess glanced up as she continued chipping away at the nail polish.

"We're all going to die. You just need to slow down the process." Dr. Andrews opened Tess's folder and studied her copy of the health evaluation report.

"Let's see what this says. You spend zero hours a week in physical activity?" she asked incredulously.

Tess looked back at her fingers as she nodded sheepishly.

"Do you exercise at all?"

Tess shrugged and shook her head.

"Clean house?"

Looking up, Tess answered that question with a grimace. "I hire a cleaning service to do that. They come in once a week."

Dr. Andrews closed the folder and tossed it on the table. "Do you garden?"

"I live in a high-rise condo. There aren't any yards."

"Do you walk your dog?"

Tess could tell the doctor was grasping at straws. "I have a cat, but I do walk to work. It's about half a mile from the condo."

"Well, at least that's a start. You could walk more. For example, do you try to park as far away as possible when you go to the grocery store?"

Tess concentrated on the next fingernail and began stripping it. "I don't have a car."

Dr. Andrews sighed. "What do you usually do for food?"

"I eat out."

"All the time?"

"Just about. Oh, except for snacks. And when I bring the leftovers home."

"You could walk to a park and eat there. Washington has lots of parks. Think of other places to walk. You could even go some place like the Smithsonian to get in your walking when the weather is bad."

"I don't have time for museums. I work."

"All of the time?"

"Most of the time."

"You need to get a life."

"I do. I have a life." Tess removed her glasses and rubbed the bridge of her nose. "I invent ice cream flavors for Amanda Rae Ice Cream."

"Say, you wouldn't be the one who dreamed up that Teddy Bear Fudge Brownie stuff, would you?"

"Yes." Tess was glad to be on safer ground.

"That is one awesome flavor. Everyone in my family loves it."

"Thank you. But I don't just invent the flavors. I'm also the head taster, which is great, because I can make sure they don't screw up my creations during production."

Beaming, Tess put her glasses back on. At least one good thing had happened during this visit. She'd met another Amanda Rae fan.

"I can't believe somebody actually gets paid for tasting ice cream. It sounds like a dream job."

"You'd be amazed how many people say that."

Picking up Tess's folder, Dr. Andrews stood, walked over to her desk, and sat down in the chair behind it. "Actually, you could be in much worse shape working with ice cream all day like you do. If I had your job, I'd be so big I couldn't fit through the door."

So the doctor obviously didn't think she was that unhealthy. Tess gave a sigh of relief.

Dr. Andrews flipped open the file again. "Don't think you're out of the woods, though. You need to concentrate on getting these numbers down. Don't worry too much about your weight. You don't have that much to lose. Besides, it will come down naturally if you start walking more and watching your fat intake." Dr. Andrews looked up. "Let's talk about diet for a while."

Unzipping her bulging leather purse, Tess fished around and pulled out a package of bubble gum. "I can't do diets. I've tried." She offered a stick to the doctor.

Dr. Andrews shook her head. "You just have to start eating the right kind of food. Maybe if you started cooking at home . . ."

"Oh, I don't cook."

"You must cook some."

"No. Not at all." Tess snapped her gum. "Oops. Sorry. My friend Lorraine teases me about my lack of cooking ability all the time. She claims that my culinary skills are so bad I have to send out for boiling water."

"And yet you create extraordinary ice cream."

"But I don't actually cook it. The lab people do that for me. Besides, I'm happy living on fast food. The nachos supreme at Tasty Taco is my idea of gourmet cuisine."

"I don't want to scare you, Tess, but you have to make some immediate changes in your diet and lifestyle or face some pretty dire health consequences. Clogged arteries. Increased risk of a stroke, not to mention a heart attack. You're definitely going to have to curtail your fast food intake. In fact, if you can't resist that ice cream you're around every day, you might even have to find another line of work."

Tess swallowed her gum. She'd die if she had to quit her job. She loved her work. She didn't want to do anything else. She was the best in the business. After all, hadn't the Amanda Rae company insured her taste buds for a million dollars? "But if I can't cook, how am I supposed to . . ."

Dr. Andrews opened the top drawer of her desk and pulled out a business card. "Here. This is a local catering firm which specializes in preparing healthy meals for busy executives. My other patients have had a lot of luck with them and keep telling me how wonderful their food is."

Tess took the card. "Pure Heart Catering? Okay. I'll give them a try. What have I got to lose?"

Chapter Three

Tess indulged herself in several days of wallowing in self pity before she decided it was time to call Pure Heart Catering. She and Lorraine had spent their last few days of gastronomical freedom eating everything that wasn't nailed down, and then some. She savored the last spoonful of her newest creation, Berry Berry Hot Fudge Delight. Now she was finally ready to start her new life in bland food limbo. Sort of. Groaning, she picked up the phone and dialed.

"Hello, Pure Heart Catering. This is Zach Ferrara speaking."

Great. Zach sounded as though he were six and a half feet of solid muscle. He probably worked out for hours every days. He probably broke the ice in the Potomac to swim. He probably . . . oh, just thinking about his physical activities made her tired.

"Hello. Is somebody there?" His voice was deep and strong.

"Hello, my name is Tess Samuels. My doctor—I mean, my company's doctor—said I should call you."

"I assume you mean Dr. Andrews."

Zach really did sound six and a half feet tall. And muscular. He probably knew what Tess weighed just by hearing her voice. Then again, maybe he was just a big, self-centered body-builder who was more interested in his own biceps than her weight.

"Hello? I asked if you were referred by Dr. Andrews . . ."

"Well, yes. She speaks very highly of your company."

"We do have the highest success rate in our field." The pride in his voice was unmistakable. "Ninty-five percent of our clients rated themselves as more than satisfied with our catering."

She couldn't help herself. "Ninty-five percent. What about the other five percent? Did they die?"

Tess heard a choking noise at the other end of the line.

"They most certainly did not die. That other five percent made the conscious choice not to succeed. Life is full of choices, you know."

Ignoring his unsolicited sermonette, Tess continued, "Dr. Andrews said that you'd make all my meals if I wanted you to."

"We can do that."

"And the meals would always be waiting for me when I got home? I'm starved at the end of the day."

"Your meals will be ready when you get home," Zach assured her.

That sounded pretty good. "All right. I've decided to give you guys a try. Can I hire you for a couple of days or so until I see whether or not I like your cooking?"

"Of course you'll like our cooking. I can provide references . . ."

"I don't care whether or not other people like what you cook. I'm the one who has to like your food if you're cooking for me." Tess knew she was starting to sound hostile, but she didn't care. Especially when this guy sounded so smug.

"We accommodate all tastes, no matter how discerning."

"That's just a nice way of saying I'm picky, isn't it?"

"Look, Ms. Samuels, perhaps you should rethink this. Maybe our service isn't the right one for you."

Tess hadn't expected that response. She needed Pure Heart Catering. Her health depended on it. Her job depended on it. Maybe she had been a little . . . abrupt.

"I'm sorry. I didn't mean to offend you. I'm just going through a difficult—"

"Tell you what," Zach interrupted. "I'll send you our food preference survey to get you started. Just fill it out and fax it back with your health history. As soon as we get the completed form, we'll work out the details."

"Before I hang up, I need to tell you something."

"Yes?"

"I don't own a single cooking pan. Not even one." Smiling, she waited for his shocked response.

It never came.

"Don't worry about it. We always bring our own. Now, if you'll give me your fax number, we'll be on our way toward making you a part of that satisfied ninty-five percent.''

He wasn't going to get his hopes up again. Chances were very good that Tess Samuels wasn't his lady in red, Zach told himself as he stood in the office of Pure Heart Catering, waiting for the last page of her fax to come through. Glancing at the first page, he snorted in disbelief. In all of his years as a nutritionist, he'd never seen such unhealthful responses to the food preference questionnaire. His lady in red would never eat like this.

At least Tess Samuels was honest. Usually people lied on this form, claiming a lifelong love of grilled swordfish, brown rice, and spinach salad without any dressing. This woman's preferences read like a catalogue of forbidden food—ice cream, pizza, nachos, and cheeseburgers.

He sat down on the edge of the desk and scanned her health history. Sky-high cholesterol. Time bomb blood pressure. Her weight had been whited out, of course. But he could guess.

According to her own responses, Tess Samuels ate more and moved less than any other person in the D.C. area. Usually the executives he dealt with were no more than thirty to forty pounds overweight. Except for the ambassador from South Africa. That guy had weighed in at close to 400 pounds, but they'd even gotten *him* into shape.

Zach knew a challenge when he saw one. He decided right then and there to tackle this case himself instead of assigning Tess to someone else on his staff. Her list of favorites—and her workaholic life-style—reminded him of his own former precoronary existence. After all, it had only been five years since he'd almost paid the ultimate price for his sixty-hour work weeks and vending machine diet.

Wandering over to his computer as he read, he sat down and began to browse his recipe files. He had a feeling that pleasing this client was going to be a tall order, but he knew he could do it. Somehow.

Tess Samuels's apartment was nothing like Zach had imagined. Except for the expensive, exclusive address, that is. He wasn't surprised that he didn't see any pictures of her on the walls—most overweight people, he had learned over the years, were camera-shy.

The condo was decorated in deep, rich colors. One of the living room walls was the same purple as a ripe eggplant. Red, purple, and black throw pillows graced the overstuffed, buttery gold leather sofa. There was nothing timid, nothing tame about this decor. Her taste in furniture and art could almost be called exotic . . . and certainly sensual. Jewel-toned woven area rugs were scattered over the dark hardwood floors.

He noticed that the many books on the recessed shelving were in several languages. French. Latin. Italian. German.

One particular bookshelf caught his eye. This one wasn't full of books, but rocks, each one on a pedestal under its own spotlight. Not rocks! he corrected himself, but gems and minerals, their colors rivaling those in the room around them.

The condo smelled as spicy as it looked. Ceramic bowls filled with potpourris of orange and cloves and cinnamon were scattered about the room.

The kitchen was as dead as the rest of the apartment was lively. White. Sterile. Unused. Neglected. Except for a pet's personalized food and water dishes, there was no color, no sign of life. Well, he was going to fix that.

Less than half an hour later, Zach stood at the counter in Tess's kitchen slicing jicama into thin strips for a southwestern salad he was preparing for her. A well-fed calico cat named Tiberia, according to her bowl, had decided Zach was her friend the minute he'd started cooking, and now she wove in and out between his legs as he worked on the salad.

The cat's food dish was empty, and she was acting hungry, so Zach figured it must be time for her to eat. He opened the cupboard doors. One full section was lined with can after can of expensive gourmet cat food, the kind you couldn't get at an ordinary grocery store. Every flavor imaginable, from Salmon Soufflé to Feast of Pheasant filled the shelves.

Curious, he opened the next set of doors to see what kind of people food this Tess Samuels kept around. Candy.

Boxes and bags and bars of it. Two shelves full, in fact. Below them sat a row of salty snacks—potato chips and corn chips and nuts. He opened the other cupboards. Not much. A few dishes and a couple of glasses.

Now Zach was really intrigued. Opening the refrigerator, he found two dozen or so bottles of drinking water and twice as many cans of soda. How could someone who had put together such a wonderfully vibrant living room have such a sorry excuse for a kitchen?

She was paying him to help her get healthy, and dammit, that's exactly what he intended to do. Grabbing a trash bag from his box of supplies, he emptied the refrigerator of the sodas and the cupboards of the junk food. Determinedly, he spun the bag, closed it with a twist tie and stepped toward the front door.

As Zach reached for the door handle, he paused and turned around. The freezer. He hadn't checked the freezer. Pivoting on his heel, he marched back into the kitchen and opened the freezer door.

There, in all their high-fat glory, sat virtually every flavor of Amanda Rae ice cream. He had always thought that this particular brand of frozen decadence should be registered as an addictive substance. He'd seen more cartons of Amanda Rae in new client's freezers than any other kind. And when his clients succumbed to temptation, they almost always went astray with Amanda Rae.

With a firm resolve, Zach chucked the contents of the freezer into another bag and headed back toward the trash chute.

When Tess arrived home, she was greeted by a cacophony of seductive food-based aromas. The new chef from Pure Heart must have beat her home. What was for dinner? She couldn't tell, but it sure smelled good.

"Anyone here?" she called.

The rattling of pans was her only response. Either

Tiberia had taken up the culinary arts or the chef was still in her apartment.

Holding their biggest competitor's newest ice cream sandwich sensation in one cold hand, she took off her winter cape, hung it on the stand by the door, and followed her nose to the kitchen. The first thing she saw when she walked into the room was Tiberia happily chowing down. Kneeling, she gave the patchwork cat a gentle stroke.

The next thing Tess noticed was the back of a tall, slender man with a dancer's build. His black turtleneck shirt and form-fitting black slacks were protected by a dark green apron. His shoulder-length blond hair was pulled back into a ponytail. Funny, she hadn't run across a lot of long-haired men for ages. And now, she'd seen two of them—first, the hunk in the elevator, and now, this guy.

He bent over to get something out of the oven, his back still to her. "Welcome home, Ms. Samuels." There was that deep voice again. This had to be the same guy who had talked to her on the phone. What was his name again? Something that started with a Z. Zane? Zeus? Zorro? He certainly looked like a blond Zorro from behind. No. Not Zorro. Zach. That was his name. Zach.

She watched as he did something to whatever he had in the oven. She'd been wrong. He obviously wasn't a body-builder, but he sure had nice buns.

Tess was shocked by her reaction to him. She usually didn't look at men's butts. Good grief. She was actually leering.

This man was too distracting. She glanced down at the floor and took another bite of ice cream, concentrating on the mix of flavors. Amanda Rae's lab people might get a chemical composition of their competitor's products, but she could pinpoint even the slightest flavor variation.

Engrossed in her analysis, she didn't look up until he started talking to her again.

"I'm Zach Ferrara." He turned around and extended his hand to her.

One look from his penetrating gray eyes, and the rest of the ice cream sandwich fell from Tess's fingers. It was *him*. The man who smelled like freshly baked bread. The man who'd held her in his arms. The man who . . .

Zach stared at her in disbelief. The lady in red. Tess Samuels was the lady in red. The gods were smiling. Tess Samuels was his new client. But that ice cream wasn't good for her.

In a move worthy of a pro basketball player, he caught the fumbled snack—and tossed it into the nearby wastebasket. He hoped she'd be impressed by his quick save.

Tess wasn't impressed. The man of her dreams was in her kitchen, and he'd just thrown away the sample of ice cream. She was this close to figuring out the secret ingredient. And after such a spectacular rescue. She could only sputter out her objections.

Finally, she found her voice. "Why did you do that?" She began digging in the trash can and defiantly fished out the remains of the ice cream treat. "I needed to analyze its flavor."

"You're not going to eat it, are you?" Zach looked as though he were ready to deep-six the sample a second time.

Holding it out of his reach, Tess peeled the chocolate cookie part from the ice cream sandwich. "Of course I can't eat this now. Not after it's been in the trash."

She slid the glob of vanilla ice cream into the cat's food bowl. "Tiberia's going to eat it. We never waste ice cream in this house. Even our competitor's."

Zach was standing only a few inches away from her and already she could feel his body heat. It tickled her skin, raising goosebumps down her neck and spine. She took a deep breath, inhaling his scent. That wonderful aroma of freshly baked bread.

"So now you're trying to ruin your cat's health, too?" Her delicious thoughts shattered.

"Excuse me? Me ruin my cat's health? What are you, another James Herriot?"

He knitted his brows. "Who's James Herriot?"

"The English veterinarian who wrote all those sweet books about those darling animals."

Ignoring her encyclopedic knowledge, he went right back to the subject of Tiberia. "It doesn't take an expert to know you shouldn't be feeding your cat high fat ice cream. It can't be any better for her than it is for you."

So this gorgeous guy was as prone to giving sermons in person as he was over the phone. Well, she didn't need this kind of aggravation, goosebumps or no goosebumps.

Ice cream. That would help calm her. She headed toward the freezer—and her special stash of Amanda Rae's. Much to her horror, it was gone. Every last carton of it.

How dare this stranger invade the sanctity of her

freezer? "What's going on? You threw out my ice cream? What gives you the right to throw out any food of mine? This wasn't in the contract!"

Zach remained annoyingly calm. "Apparently you didn't read the fine print. We're supposed to eliminate any unhealthy food from the premises and replace it with things that are good for you."

"I read every word of that contract, and that wasn't in it."

"Well, it should be."

"It's obvious to me that you're the wrong person for this job. I'm calling your boss right now and asking for someone else." She reached for the phone. "What's Pure Heart's phone number?"

So his lady in red wanted to fire him. "Let me get this straight. You want *me* to give *you* the phone number when you're planning to use it to get me fired? Right." He began to laugh.

She put her hands on her hips, drawing his attention to her luscious curves. "I don't see what's so funny. You're about to join the ranks of the unemployed."

He expected to see her stomp her foot at any minute. "There's no way I'll get fired from Pure Heart."

"We'll just see about that. Now, what's their number?"

He was so glad to have found his lady in red that he didn't care how ticked off she was. Besides, the fire in her amber-colored eyes made her all the more desirable. He told her the number, and added, "But don't bother calling. The boss isn't there."

"The boss isn't there?" She reached for the phone. "And just how do you know that?"

"Because the boss is here."

"Where?" She looked around.

"In your kitchen. Preparing you a healthy, delicious meal." Chuckling, he picked up the cat dish and rinsed it out.

So much for reporting him to his supervisor. She'd just have to fire him directly.

"Well, pack up your things and leave. Now."

She watched as Zach put the cat dish back on the floor. He didn't seem to be paying any attention to her. She tapped him on the shoulder. "Hey, I'm talking to you."

Touching him was a mistake. The instant she came in contact with him, her traitorous body remembered how good it had felt when he'd held her.

He studied her for a long moment.

Those gorgeous gray eyes. And that damned eyebrow. He was raising it again. It made her feel warm to the tips of her toes.

"You were saying?"

And his voice. It flowed over her like hot fudge.

"Where was I? Oh, yes. You need to leave."

"But you haven't eaten yet. Don't you at least want to try what I've cooked for you before you let me go?"

"Okay. But I've ... I've decided to give another caterer a try."

"Oh? Which one?"

He smiled, and she knew he'd probably win this battle. "Never mind."

"That's very gracious of you." He grinned as he fed her cat a morsel of salmon.

"Maybe I'll give you another chance. After all, my

cat seems to like you. Normally, she doesn't have any use for strangers. I wouldn't want to upset Tiberia, of course."

"Of course." He went back to working on the salad.

Zach didn't say a word. He finished crumbling the grilled salmon onto the salad, washed his hands, and took off his apron.

Tess tried not to notice Zach's muscular chest as he loaded his ingredients and all the dishes he'd used into a plastic box. It didn't work.

"I've set the dining room table. Your breakfast and brown bag lunch are in the fridge. Hope you enjoy them."

She could see the outline of his biceps as he lifted the box.

When Zach reached the door, he shifted the box to one arm and turned the knob. "Good night, Ms. Samuels." He nodded his farewell. "Eat well."

What a waste of a perfectly fine body on such a presumptuous man. "Ice cream assassin," Tess muttered as she double-locked the door behind him.

Chapter Four

Zach smiled when he heard the rapid slam of the door behind him and the telltale clicks of two locks being hastily secured. Tess Samuels was making sure he didn't change his mind and go back into her apartment again this evening. He wouldn't have minded spending a little more time with his argumentative client, but apparently, she had other plans.

She didn't look anything at all the way he'd pictured her. After reading her profile and seeing the stockpile of snacks in her kitchen, he'd expected her to be incredibly overweight. Tess had to have one helluva metabolism, because all she had were some very, very nice curves.

Now that his curiosity was satisfied, he really should turn the preparation of her meals over to someone on his staff who actually was supposed to do it. But not just yet, he told himself.

Whistling, he pushed the down button on the elevator. He still couldn't believe that Tess Samuels and the lady in red were one and the same. It was obviously a sign. He intended to get to know her—with or without her cooperation. It was going to be interesting either way.

Tess gave a sigh of relief as she double-locked the door after Zach. She kicked off her pumps and headed for the dining room and the meal he'd prepared. She hoped it tasted as wonderful as it smelled. It certainly looked delicious.

She picked a piece of salmon from the salad and popped it into her mouth. Heavenly. She had no idea fish could taste this good, although Tiberia always seemed to enjoy it. But then, Ti also enjoyed eating moths and crickets, so it was obvious her cat wasn't much of a food critic.

Sighing happily, Tess sat down and unrolled her napkin. A piece of paper fell into her lap. When she picked it up, she noticed a message scrawled across it. The penmanship, if you could call it that, was the worst she'd ever seen. She stared at the paper, trying to decipher it, squinting as she attempted to read it aloud.

Maybe her glasses were smudged. As she took them off and wiped them with the napkin, Ti jumped up on the chair next to her to see what all the excitement was about.

"I don't know what to say, Ti." She put her glasses back on, sighing when it didn't change the way the writing looked on the note. "I can read Italian and Latin and French, even the old kind, but this is . . ."

She held out the paper to the fascinated feline. "Well, can *you* tell what this says?"

Tiberia, who'd began a hasty retreat as soon as the note fluttered in front of her face, offered no help.

Tess studied the first word. Two letters and a big slash. Suddenly it became clear what the word was. An "m" with four humps, an "s" with more straight lines than curves, and a fat line for a period. She began to feel like the archaeologist who had just broken the code to the Dead Sea Scrolls.

Looking for other familiar letters, Tess finally deciphered more of the note. *Ms. Samuels, please let me know if you enjoyed the* . . . She tried forming the next word with her mouth. "Slime." Slime? No, that had to be wrong. Salary? Slave? Salute? None of them fit or made sense, and this word didn't follow any of the shapes of the previous ones. She looked around the room for a clue. "Salad." Of course it was salad.

Triumphantly, she read on. *The first few* . . . The first few what? Dogs? No. That couldn't be it. "Days." *The first few days are always the hardest.* She was on a roll. *Here is my cell phone number.*

In the midst of all the chicken scratch writing were seven perfectly formed numbers. The contrast made her giggle. *Call in case you're having trouble* . . .

There was no way she could read the next four words. They probably weren't that important anyway. She skipped ahead. *In the meantime, there's a train for you in your refrigerator.*

A train in the refrigerator? Now Tess was really curious. Pushing back her chair, she picked another piece of salmon from the salad and headed toward the kitchen. There, on the refrigerator, was a magnet shaped like a heart declaring, *Pure Heart Catering. We care what you eat.*

After consigning the magnet to the same fate as her ice cream, she opened the refrigerator. Zach had left her not a train, but a tray. A tray filled with flowers—radish roses, celery blooms, and a sunflower made out of orange segments and raisins. Her soda pop had disappeared, a case of expensive mineral water taking its place. She wanted caffeine and sugar, not an edible floral shop. Closing the refrigerator door in disgust, she returned to her meal, only to find Tiberia standing in the middle of the table munching happily on the salmon salad.

"Oh, Ti! I should have known not to leave you and fish alone together in the same room." The cat flicked her tail in agreement. "Well, enjoy." She picked up Ti and the salad bowl and set them both on the floor.

The only thing left for Tess to eat for supper was the vegetarian bouquet. She didn't even want to look inside the two brown bags marked with happy-face "Breakfast" and "Lunch" stickers. With a heartfelt sigh, Tess went back to the kitchen to retrieve the tray of fat-free snacks Zach had so artfully arranged. Setting them on the counter, she ate the orange segments first, right off the platter. But it only took a couple of mouthfuls of the rest of the healthy respite to figure out that the vegetables looked prettier than they tasted. Ranch-style dip sure would have helped. Of course, her healthy hero hadn't left any of that.

As Tess contemplated whether to try a broccoli floret or a carrot curl next, a third option popped into her mind. She opened her cupboard doors. Zach had cleared out every last pretzel, chip, candy bar, and jelly bean. The only food left was fit for a cat. Literally. Sorry that Zach's head wasn't between the cupboard doors, she slammed them shut.

She hoped he hadn't searched the whole condo. There was still that box of caramel pecan clusters in her nightstand drawer that she hadn't gotten to yet. Now *that* would be a substantial meal. Gleefully, she dumped the beautiful vegetables into the trash can, tossed the tray on the counter, and headed for her room.

"Hold still, Phoebe. I can't rinse the bubbles off you when you're wiggling like that." Zach tested the temperature of the hand-held spray, being careful not to soak the blue striped wallpaper in his bathroom the way he had the day before. "I know, I know. You really like it when I do this."

Zach watched as the dirt from his prize-winning garden ran in rivulets down to the drain. Phoebe had turned his life upside down in less than a month's time, but a promise was a promise. After all, no one else was willing to take the tiny potbellied pig when his administrative assistant, Nan, had to give her up.

Phoebe grunted and squealed in protest when he finally turned off the water.

"You're a slippery little devil, aren't you? And don't try to get away from me like you did last night. It was midnight before I got all those wet piggy prints mopped up. In other words, don't even think about trying to escape—I'm not letting you out of here until I've dried you off."

Zach tossed a thick towel over the struggling animal

and knelt beside her. Gently, he patted the pig's face and snout dry. "You won't believe this, Phoebe. You know that woman in red? The one I was telling you about the other day? Guess what? I found her."

Phoebe stopped squirming and appeared to be listening intently. She perked up her ears.

"I knew you'd be surprised, too." He gave her one last pat. "All done. Time to put you to bed."

The young pig trotted down the hallway to her fuschia blanket in the corner of the living room and burrowed under it. Zach settled into his favorite easy chair, picked up his laptop computer, and began to plan menus for his clients for the following week.

When he got to Tess's file, he paused. Should he bother planning her meals that far in advance? Would she have the willpower to make it through even one week of healthy eating?

Opening the file, he began to type. He'd plan menus for Tess Samuels for the next week. Hell, he'd plan them for the next month. Now that she was officially a client, there was no way he'd let her ruin his track record.

Tess woke up to the unfamiliar sound of her stomach growling. She picked up the waterproof watch Lorraine had given her for her last birthday from the nightstand and looked at the glowing numbers. Two o'clock. Not bothering with slippers, she padded to the kitchen and opened the refrigerator door.

The light in the refrigerator and the light in her head went on at the same time. Of course she was starving to death. The caramel pecan clusters she'd wolfed down for supper hadn't filled her up, and now she only had these two dumb brown paper bags to choose from. And it was all *his* fault. Zach Ferrara had destroyed her food supply and had probably left her with two sacks full of alfalfa sprouts and goat's milk. She turned up her nose at the thought.

Her stomach continued to growl. Deciding that something, no matter how disgustingly healthy and inedible it was, had to be better than nothing, she reached for the bag labeled "Breakfast." With a sigh of deep resignation, she broke the happy-face seal and dumped the contents onto her kitchen counter. A small red apple, a good-sized muffin, and a pint container of skim milk fell out along with a red, heart-shaped note card.

With blurry eyes, she read the message. Thank goodness it was typed. *Congratulations! You've taken the first step on that important journey to a healthy life.* Making an exasperated snort, she wadded up the note and lobbed it toward the wastebasket.

The muffin didn't look that bad. It was large, and more importantly, it looked so dark and scrumptious that it had to be chocolate. Excitedly, Tess ripped off the cellophane, took a big bite, and almost gagged. The muffin was the nastiest thing she'd ever eaten. Grainy and gritty and gross.

She grabbed the milk carton and fumbled with the carton's spout—she had to get that revolting taste out of her mouth. One more giant tug, and the carton came open with a splash. Milk flew up in her face and covered her purple satin pajamas. Ignoring the mess, she gulped down what little liquid was left. At the sound of the unexpected feast, Tiberia jumped onto the counter and proceeded to lap up as much milk as she could.

Tess pushed her soggy hair out of her face with an angry swipe of her hand. She was still hungry, and to top everything off, now she had to take a shower, change, and mop up the spilled milk. Grabbing the apple, she took a vicious bite as she headed toward the bathroom.

After her shower, Tess sat on the edge of her bed drying her hair with a plush emerald green towel. Tomorrow she'd give that Zach a piece of her mind. Or better yet, a piece of the muffin. Talk about a taste of your own medicine. That would show him.

Why wait until tomorrow? After all, it was tomorrow. At least it was two and a half hours into tomorrow. Smiling, she picked up the phone.

Zach groaned as he reached for the receiver. It couldn't be morning yet. He forced open one eye and peered at the numbers on his clock radio. Two-thirty. Who in the world would be calling him at two-thirty in the morning? It had to be a wrong number. "Hello?"

"Good morning, Zach!" a bright, cheery voice answered. "I hope I didn't wake you up."

"Who is this?"

"You don't know who this is? How can you possibly run a successful business when you don't recognize your own customers?"

Zach turned on the lamp by the bed, knocking the phone off the nightstand. He leaned over the edge of the bed, using one hand to pull the phone by the cord toward him. He was breathing heavily by the time he rolled back on the mattress. He put the base of the phone on his chest and cradled the receiver next to his ear. "Is this Tess Samuels? Do you have any idea what time it is?"

"2:35, if my watch is correct. Why are you whispering?"

Raising his voice several notches, he barked, "I'm not whispering. What do you want?"

"I just wanted to tell you how much I enjoyed that breakfast you left for me."

Zach thought he heard Phoebe waking up in the next room. He lowered his voice. "Can't you call me later?"

"You left me a note telling me to call you anytime."

"I didn't mean that literally."

"So your company makes a habit of lying to their customers?"

"No . . . okay, I guess I did say that. But I meant call me during waking hours."

"I'm awake."

"Normal waking hours." Zach heard the sound of pig trotters on the tile in the hallway, then porcine grunting. "Oh no, now look what you've done. Phoebe's awake, and I'm never going to get her back to bed again."

"Well, if you've forced her to eat your muffins, I can see why you're having trouble getting her back into your bed. Your muffins stink."

His protest cut off as she hung up the phone; he stared at the receiver. "You like my muffins, don't you, girl?"

As Phoebe grunted her agreement, he dialed the number on his caller ID.

Tess answered on the second ring. "Who is this? Don't you know what time it is?"

"My muffins don't stink." Satisfied that he had set the record straight, Zach hung up the phone, picked up Phoebe, and carried her back to her bed.

Chapter Five

It was all Zach's fault that Tess couldn't sleep. If he hadn't called her back just to get in the last word, she could have taken the first boat out to dreamland. Instead, she'd lain awake trying to think of another last word. It never came.

Tess had just dozed off when her alarm rang. She didn't even have time to turn it off before Tiberia leaped up on her pillow, demanding her breakfast. "Just five more minutes. Okay, pretty kitty?" Tess pulled the satin comforter over her head. Undaunted, the insistent cat tunneled under the covers and howled in her right ear.

"All right. All right." Tess forced herself out of bed, putting on her glasses as she slid her feet into her quilted slippers. The hungry cat danced around her as she shuffled her way into the kitchen.

Tess nudged Tiberia away from the electric can opener as she opened her cat food. "You'd think you hadn't eaten in a million years." She laughed as the cat tried to scoop out the food with her paw before the bowl even hit the ground. "And you know you had a midnight snack."

As she took the empty can over to the wastebasket, something squished under her foot. Frowning, she took off her slipper to see what was attached to it. Something brown and disgusting.

"Tiberia?"

Funny, the cat didn't look guilty.

Then she noticed the cellophane stuck to the bottom of the brown stuff. The muffin strikes again, she thought, tossing the soiled slipper into the trash. She looked around the kitchen. Stray pieces of vegetables littered the floor where she had missed the garbage can the night before. Obviously Tiberia'd had a great time after Tess went to bed. The kitchen island was covered with bits of brown paper bag and shredded napkin. The ripped, empty milk carton was punctured by what could only have been sharp little cat teeth.

"Looks like you had yourself quite a party, Ti. I should leave this mess for our friend Zach, but you'll probably expand your play area to the living room if I do." Sighing, Tess bent over and began to clean up the floor.

It seemed to take forever, and Tess had little time left to get ready for work. Hoping that her early morning shower was still good, she pulled a turquoise velour dress out of her closet. She wriggled into her body-sculpting pantyhose, the ones guaranteed to make her look ten pounds thinner. Halfway up, she thought she'd lost the circulation in her thighs. Taking a deep breath, she inched them the rest of the way on. It felt as though she were wearing a giant rubber band around her waist.

Next, she struggled into her longline bra. Apparently, the line wasn't long enough, because a stubborn roll of soft flesh appeared where the bra was supposed to meet the pantyhose. Groaning with the effort, she pulled the waistband of the pantyhose higher, constricting her body even further.

Despite the morning chill, Tess had begun to do some serious perspiring. She mopped her damp face with a couple of tissues before pulling on her satiny slip and dress. Tess looked at herself in the mirror and smiled. Who needed a diet when she had miracle pantyhose? Now if she could only breathe. . . .

The entire research and development staff was crowded around the receptionist's desk when Tess arrived at the office fifteen minutes late. "Did somebody bring goodies?" she asked Lorraine as she joined the group.

"Girlfriend, you've just got to try one of these." Her friend picked a muffin out of the basket, curling her hand around it delicately, ever mindful of her long, lacquered nails. "They're fantastic."

Lorraine passed her the muffin. Tess stared in horror at the familiar, cellophane-covered brown lump in her hand. It couldn't be. . . .

Tess looked around the room. Sure enough, there was Zach, standing in the corner, watching the feeding frenzy. His arms were crossed over his chest, and he had the most self-satisfied expression she'd ever seen on a fellow human being.

"Tell me what's going on here," she demanded as she marched toward him, holding the muffin like a hand grenade.

"I'm just doing some unbiased taste testing," he responded, lifting his hand to acknowledge Lorraine's thanks before she returned to her office. He walked over to the desk and retrieved the now empty basket. "Apparently, you were wrong." He turned over the basket to make his point. "My muffins don't stink."

Setting the basket upright, she dropped the unwanted muffin back into it. "Some taste test. Research and development people will eat anything, as long as it's free. What did you do? Spend all night making these things?"

He cleared his throat. "Well, since I was already awake . . ."

"So how did Phoebe feel about you playing bake-off?"

"Phoebe likes it when I bake. She's a pig."

What kind of a guy would refer to the woman he lived with as a pig? "Sounds to me like the romance is over."

"No, you don't understand. Phoebe really *is* a pig."

Before she could make her point, Lucas from the office down the hall interrupted their conversation. "Those were the best bran muffins I've ever had. What's your secret?"

"It's my own recipe. Molasses bran."

She couldn't believe that Zach would actually take pride in something that looked like it belonged on the floor of a stable, but there he was, beaming as though he had good sense.

"Phoebe loves them," he added.

"Molasses bran? Phoebe has no taste, either," Tess muttered as Lucas walked away. "You're never going to believe what I thought your muffin was this morning. Let's just say I threw away my slipper when I stepped in it."

"You stepped on my muffin?" The look on his face was priceless. "Isn't that a rather extreme way to express your dislike for my baking?"

"Oh, stepping on it didn't even begin to express my opinion of your muffins."

"Well, if you hate my muffins so much, why are you taking a chance on bringing that lunch I fixed for you?"

She tried to hide the brown paper sack behind her.

He grinned at her attempt to conceal the damning evidence. "Well?"

"I'm starving, and this was all that I had in the house to eat." Tess narrowed her eyes. "Thanks to you."

"I left you a huge tray of fresh vegetables, and the salmon salad should have been more than enough to fill you up at supper."

How could this man possibly know what satisfied her appetite? "I don't have to justify to anyone, especially you, what I did or didn't eat." Was that shrill voice really hers?

Zach, curse his tofu-loving heart, remained calm. "Look, I need to know what you like and don't like, so I don't keep wasting your money on food you're just going to throw away." He paused. "Or step on."

"I faxed you that list of what I like to eat. Why aren't you using that?"

"You and I both know those things aren't healthy. I'm supposed to cure you, not kill you. But I can't help you unless I know what you're willing to eat."

If he insisted on being dense, she'd have to spell it out. "Okay. The salad was . . . fine. But the vegetables needed something—like dip. And those darned bran muffins of yours had better never darken my doorway again."

"Got it. Salad's a go. Dress up the veggies. Lose the muffins. Although you really should give them another chance . . ."

"Not in this lifetime. They taste like dirt. Kill the muffins."

"All right. The muffins die. I'll see if we can do better tonight."

He turned to leave.

"Wait!"

"Yes?"

"There aren't any muffins in here, are there?" She jiggled the bag.

"No. You're safe. But you still need to have a lunch if you're eating that for breakfast. I'll send something by for you around noon."

If he weren't such a food fanatic, Zach Ferrara would be kind of cute. "Thanks."

"Don't thank me yet."

"I'm telling you, Tess, you're so far out of circulation that you don't recognize a prime-cut male when you see one."

"Rainey, would you get your fanny off my report so I can finish reading this analysis?" Tess poked her friend with the end of her pen.

As Lorraine scooted to the middle of the desk, Tess pulled the papers out from under her.

"For years, you've tried to fix me up with every Tom, Dick, and Harry that's come within fifty yards of this office. I've tried to ignore it when you drag them in here and say, 'Have you met my friend, Tess? She's single.' Real subtle, Rainey. But I'm not going to let you cook up a romance between me and the granola gourmet."

"What's wrong with him? He's gorgeous. He cooks. He waits on you. He cleans. He's employed. What more do you want? If I didn't have my own personal sugar bear I'd go after that man myself. He's too good to waste."

"I don't care about all that. You know what my idea of an ideal man is . . ."

"Boring."

"I never said such a thing."

"But I did."

"I want a man . . ."

Her friend interrupted. "I know, I know. You want a man with the I.Q. of Einstein. One who can stimulate you intellectually. One who can understand what you're reading when you recite one of those dull old Latin poems."

Lorraine rolled her eyes as though the very thought of such a male disgusted her. "Girl, I'm here to tell you that if your man doesn't show a little intelligence and imagination in the bedroom, he's not worth a hill of beans. It doesn't matter whether or not he speaks Latin or understands any of those other moldy-oldie things you're so fond of quoting. It only matters that he's fluent in the language of love."

"My first boyfriend tried to teach me the language of love, and I'm here to tell you, it isn't worth speaking."

"So you had a bad first experience."

"Bad doesn't even begin to describe it. All I know is that, as far as I'm concerned, once is more than enough. Sex is highly overrated."

"Frank and I think that you just need to meet the right man," her friend said smugly.

"Please, Rainey. Do you have to discuss my sex life—or lack thereof—with Frank?"

"Honey, you've got to be kidding. When it comes to sex, the *last* thing I want to do with my sugar bear is talk about you. Or anybody else, for that matter."

The aroma of freshly baked bread wafted from Zach's kitchen through the doorway to his living room. He wrinkled his nose in pleasure and grinned as Phoebe scrambled from her mat and scuffled toward the source of the delicious scent.

He followed her into the kitchen. He didn't need a timer. The little pig always knew when the bread was ready. "Well, it looks like my luck's finally changed, Phoebe. I find my lady in red, and presto—my bread is nice and fluffy. And my muffins are a hit. With everyone but her, that is."

Phoebe snorted in disgust and nudged Zach's leg.

"I know, girl. You got to eat all of my disasters and so you're not happy about this whole successful baking thing. But you can be happy for me, can't you?''

The pig snorted again.

"Well, since you put it that way, maybe you can have just a little bit.''

Zach crumbled a warm hunk of bread into her bowl, and Phoebe practically beamed. If only Tess was so easy to please, he thought ruefully.

Chapter Six

As she walked into her kitchen, Tess knew why Zach smelled like bread. Sticking her face so close to the loaf of homemade bread that she almost touched it, she inhaled deeply, ignoring the fact that her glasses were fogging up from the steam. Who knew that bread could smell this good and still be legal? Zach promised her that his ten-grain bread was on her diet plan. As long as she left off the butter.

It was hard to believe that the same guy who'd created the muffins from hell could come up with something this heavenly.

Zach tapped her on the shoulder. "Want to taste it?"

"Oh, yeah."

He broke off a piece of the still warm bread. "Open up."

Automatically, Tess opened her mouth. She was already salivating like a starving dog. As she leaned forward, her gaze met his. Fascinated, she watched as his eyes followed the path of the bread all the way to her waiting mouth. Tenderly, he fed her, and as she closed her mouth and began to chew, he brushed a wayward crumb from her lower lip.

His attentions were tantalizing, seductive. They made her feel sexy as hell, bringing her dormant sensuality to sudden life. A glorious shiver of wanting ran through her. He ran his thumb up her jawline with a touch as light as a feather.

An annoying sound interrupted her moment of bliss. The noise went on and on. "What is that?" Tess shook her head in irritation.

Zach couldn't believe his rotten luck. What a time for the buzzer on the stove to go off. "It's the timer. It means I have to take the chicken out of the oven."

With a frustrated sigh, he turned from Tess. He pulled the baked chicken out of the oven and set it on the counter.

Zach saw Tess close her eyes as she caught a whiff of the garlic and onions. "Ummm. That smells almost as good as Tasty Taco, but not quite as good as your bread."

"Tasty Taco?" He groaned. "I'll overlook that remark and see that you get fed anyway. After all, you and I have a contract. And I never break a contract."

"Oh, yeah. That all-important ninty-five percent satisfaction rating."

He nodded. Before he'd met Tess, his catering company had been the most important thing in the world to him, but every time he looked at her, it started to seem more like a distant second.

"So . . . what are you doing this weekend that you

can't cook my food? I was sort of getting used to you. A little."

"Yeah, I know." Zach began to slice the meat off the chicken. "I grow on people, but I promised Phoebe that we'd spend tomorrow in the park."

"You mean Phoebe the pig? How can a nice guy like you call his girlfriend a pig?"

Okay, he'd try again to explain his pet. "I'm telling you, Phoebe is a real pig. A potbellied pig."

"You actually *do* have a pig? Do you live on a farm?"

"No. The pig is as close as I get to the rural life. Phoebe and I share a town house in Georgetown. There's no farm, only a very small backyard which used to have a prize-winning garden before she made herself at home."

"Why in the world did you pick a pig for your pet? Wouldn't a goldfish or a cat make more sense in a town house? And your garden would still be intact."

On cue, Tiberia strolled into the room, headed for Tess. Ignoring Tess's wiggling fingers, the cat changed course and headed straight for Zach.

"Just be patient. You know I always share the food with you." Zach smiled at Ti.

"Like I was saying, why a pig? Cats are the only perfect pet."

Tiberia meowed in agreement.

"Oh, I didn't choose Phoebe. I inherited her."

"Someone left her to you in their will?"

"No. My administrative assistant, Nan, got a new landlord who hates animals. He gave her an ultimatum—lose the pig or lose the town house. There was no way Nan could move, and I just couldn't stand by and let Phoebe go to the pound."

"Wow. That's so nice."

Zach tried not to look too pleased with himself. "You would have done the same."

"I don't know about that. It takes a special person to rescue an animal."

Her admiration warmed him like a roaring fire.

"So, you really are taking Phoebe to the park tomorrow?"

"Yes, pigs need lots of exercise and fresh air." Looking at Tess's gorgeous face and her adoring smile, he knew he didn't want to spend the next day without her. "Say, I have an idea. Why don't you come with us?"

"As in speaking of pigs . . . why don't you come with us?" Tess laughed, her eyes sparkling with merriment.

"That didn't come out right, did it?" He gave her a wry grin. "As in why don't you come with us because you're a fascinating woman, and we'd love to spend the day with you."

"Well, since you put it that way . . ." She reached over to pick off a piece of the steaming chicken, brushing her hand against the edge of the red-hot pan.

"Ow!" Tess put her hand to her mouth, nursing the small burn.

Zach pulled her around the counter, and shoved her hand under a stream of cool running tap water. He stood behind her, his body pressed up against hers, and for a moment, he forgot all about her injury. It felt so good to hold her, even if it was for first aid . . . again.

As he stood behind Tess, running the water over her small, soft hand, he wasn't able to resist the temptation to move in just a little bit closer. Her hair smelled like chocolate-covered cherries. Now he knew. He hadn't been imagining it that first day in the elevator.

A loud meow stirred him from his memories. He turned just in time to see Tiberia make a running leap for the chicken. Instinctively, Zach grabbed the pan, burning himself in the process.

The pan of chicken fell from his hands and slammed down on the floor. "Damn. I can't believe I did that."

"At least it landed right side up." Tess snatched the potholders and put the pan on the stove. "Let me see your hands."

Gently, Tess took his wrists and guided his hands under the still-running tap water. She noticed how long his fingers were. He had an artist's hands. Hands meant for creating. The perfect hands for loving. When she looked up at him, she saw a world of questions in his dove gray eyes.

She stepped back. Some questions were better left unanswered.

Zach reached for the potholders. "I'd ... uh ... I'd better get back to the chicken before the cat tries to get to it again."

"Ah, yes. The chicken."

Silently, she watched as Zach finished slicing the tender meat. He pulled a festive, hand-painted plate out of his box. Its vivid hues of gold and red and purple were identical to those in her living room. Zach had to have picked it out especially for her. The colors were too close to be a coincidence. He placed the dish on the counter and set a whole wheat tortilla in the middle of it.

"Are you sure this is Mexican food? Tasty Taco doesn't have brown tortillas."

"Just wait." He layered the chicken on the tortilla, adding chopped tomatoes, shredded lettuce, and green onions.

"There's no cheese or sour cream."

"With my homemade salsa, you'll never even notice that they're missing."

"Right." As if chunky tomatoes could make up for cheese.

Zach smiled as he topped his creation with a dollop of yogurt and a sprinkling of brilliantly green cilantro.

"If you'll be so kind as to go sit at the table, I'll bring you your supper."

He arrived at the table with the Mexican food and a bowl of melon balls just as Tess was unrolling her napkin.

He waited until she spread the napkin across her lap. "Go ahead. Take a bite."

She wondered if it mattered to him on more than a professional level that she liked his cooking.

Tentatively, she stuck her fork into the chicken and took a nibble of the meat. She closed her eyes, savoring the unfamiliar flavor. "Ummm. Heavenly." She took a bigger bite and chewed slowly. "Almost as good as Tasty Taco."

He narrowed his eyes at her. "About that trip to the park tomorrow."

"Well, maybe I could wait until tomorrow night to finish that report . . ."

"Great. I'll see you bright and early, then."

As he left the condo, Tess realized she'd forgotten to ask him exactly what time "bright and early" was.

The Mexican food was pretty good. Better than she'd thought it would be, Tess had to admit, if only to herself. And what a pretty plate. She'd eaten every bite, even the last shred of lettuce. As she scooped up a melon ball, she remembered how proud Zach seemed to have been when he made her supper. She wondered why he'd asked her to go with him to the park. He probably just thought she could use the exercise. Which she could, but he didn't need to see her break into a sweat.

She knew she was attracted to Zach, but a handsome face, great body, and excellent culinary skills were nothing to start a relationship with. Well, maybe the culinary skills were ... After all, she and Zach seemed to have very little in common. Except a love of animals.

Munching on the last melon ball, she carefully picked up the plate. Once again a note fell from it. This one was printed in fairly legible block letters. *No more molasses bran muffins. Cross my heart. But I won't make any promises about the vegetables ...*

She smiled as she took the plate to the kitchen. Normally, she'd just rinse it off and leave the real cleaning for Zach, per his contract. But this plate was special. It was so beautiful. Almost like eating from a jeweled dish. After washing and drying it as though it were a fragile gemstone, she put it in her kitchen cabinet where Tiberia wouldn't accidentally knock it down.

Closing the cabinet door, she looked around the kitchen. What an unappealing room. Why hadn't she noticed how cold it looked before? She needed—what were those things called that you put sugar and flour in?—canisters. She smiled as she came up with the right word. Not bad for a cooking impaired person.

She didn't intend to actually use the canisters, but they'd make the counter look better. And new linens. That would make the kitchen prettier, too. That's what she'd do after their walk tomorrow. Buy some nice, bright dishtowels and tablecloths for the kitchen. She'd spent hours picking out just the right colors for the linens in the bedroom and bath. Maybe she should invest a little time in these, too.

And as she turned out the light and left the kitchen, she wondered what colors Zach would like best.

Chapter Seven

The next morning, Tess woke up exhausted. She'd stayed up half the night reading a book of Renaissance love poems in the original Italian. When she finally fell asleep, she'd dreamt of Zach. Her lips formed a smile as she remembered her dream—how he'd brought her trays full of glacé and chocolate-covered biscotti as she presided at a marble table in her Italian villa. Maybe the way to a woman's heart was through her stomach. She closed her eyes as other images floated through her mind.

She stretched languorously and looked at the time. Six o'clock. She'd better get up. Zach might show up as early as seven, and she didn't want to make him wait. As she slipped her leg over the edge of the bed, the doorbell rang.

So this was Zach's idea of "bright and early." And it was still dark outside. She threw on her robe, grabbed a hairbrush, and ran it through her hair.

After a quick peek in the mirror, she headed for the living room.

Tiberia was waiting at the door, as if she were expecting company. Tess stepped over her and peered out the peephole in the door. Sure enough, she saw Zach smiling back at her. She opened the door.

"Zach, what are you doing here so early?" Immediately, Tiberia began hissing and Tess never knew what hit her. Somehow, Tess ended up on the floor when something slammed into her legs like a miniature Mack truck. The assault on her continued as something ran across her chest.

Zach yelled "Stop!" as he leaped over her prone body into the apartment. Tiberia, perched on top of a bookshelf, hissed, growled and glared. And there was Zach, desperately trying to catch a little pig running around her living room wearing a blue striped rugby sweater, its leather leash dragging behind it. At least Tess thought it was a pig. Her glasses had disappeared in the melee.

Tess pulled herself up to a sitting position and felt her chest to see if anything was broken or punctured. It wasn't easy being the hit-and-run victim of a speeding cat and a runaway pig. And in her own living room, no less. Lorraine was never going to believe this.

Just as Tess was fairly sure she had survived the onslaught with relatively minor damage, Phoebe decided to turn into a lap pig. Tess's lap pig.

At the moment of impact, Tess's grunt sounded amazingly like Phoebe's.

"Hang on to her. Don't let her get loose again," Zach called from across the room.

Tess sat very still with her arms at her sides. "She doesn't bite, does she?"

"Only if she thinks you're edible."

"Oh, great."

Phoebe rolled over, exposing a pink, hairless belly. "What's she doing now?"

"Making friends. She just wants you to rub her tummy."

"I don't think so. We haven't been properly introduced yet."

"You're afraid of a helpless little pig?"

"Little? Your helpless little pig ran across my chest with her fifty-pound body while I was stretched out on the floor. I'm lucky she didn't break every rib I have."

Phoebe grunted.

"That's right, Phoebe. You only weigh thirty pounds," Zach answered. "Females are sensitive about their weight, you know."

Tess rolled her eyes. She continued sitting on the floor, pig in lap, arms out to the side. "Please get your pig off of me."

"If you rub her belly, she'll leave on her own."

"When?"

"After she's decided you've patted her enough."

Tess gave the pig two quick pats. "That's enough. Now get off so I can find my glasses."

Much to Tess's surprise, Phoebe complied.

Zach got a firm grip on the leash. "Just stay calm."

Tess wasn't sure whether he was talking to her or his pet.

Reaching down with his other hand, Zach helped Tess up off the floor. He noticed that her hair was loose and full. Now that her glasses were missing, Zach could see that Tess's eyelashes were thick and long, the perfect frame for her bourbon-colored eyes. Best of all, her robe had somehow gotten undone, and her silky, clinging nightgown was a bright, daring red. The woman looked and smelled good enough to eat. It was already a good morning.

"Your pig has parked itself on my foot. Would you mind getting her off and helping me find my glasses?"

Zach tugged on the leash. Phoebe resisted.

"I don't understand. Normally, she's a perfectly well-behaved pig."

"Tiberia and I must bring out the worst in her."

Zach picked up the pig and tucked her under his arm. As he began stroking Phoebe behind the ears, she snuggled right up against him.

Tess could tell that this was a familiar and favorite position for both of them. The pig stared unwaveringly at her from under Zach's arm. It was almost as though the pig were telling Tess that Zach belonged to her.

A jealous pig? Was Tess going crazy? It wasn't as if she and Zach had ever done anything or even thought about doing anything remotely romantic. Unless the pig could read her mind . . . Tess looked up at Zach, wondering what he was thinking right now.

Zach was definitely watching her, not Phoebe. It made her feel funny—warm and goosebumpy at the same time. His long golden hair, which had come free during all the excitement, gave him a wildly dangerous look.

Nervously, she pressed her lips together and squinted her eyes, trying to get a better focus. His gaze appeared to be riveted on her mouth.

"So, are you going to get ready or what?" he asked, his attention still on her mouth.

"Do I have a choice?"

"Personally, I think you look pretty great just like that. But it could get kind of chilly." His grin had a distinctly wicked edge to it.

Tess looked down to see what he was staring so intently at. Oh, no. In all of the excitement she'd forgotten that she wasn't dressed yet. The darned pig had managed to undo her robe, exposing her slinky, satin nightgown. At least it was ankle-length. The actual length didn't matter, she corrected herself, when she noticed that the gown was hiked up above her knees. Hastily, she pulled her robe closed in front, cinching it together with a death grip.

With as much dignity as she could muster, Tess double-knotted the belt to her robe. As she stood, she pulled the hem down. "Well, since you came all this way . . . but I can't go anywhere until we find my glasses."

She gave a sigh of relief as Zach broke his stare and began looking around the room. "Over here. Under the coat rack." Without dropping Phoebe, he picked up the glasses and handed them to Tess.

"Thanks." She turned them over in her hand. "I don't know how it happened, but they appear to have survived intact."

"Great. Let's go."

"I really do need to put on something . . . warmer."

"If you have to."

"I have to. By the way, where are we going?" she called over her shoulder on her way to the bedroom.

"How about the C & O Canal?"

"Sounds like a plan. Make yourself at home—I should be out in ten or fifteen minutes."

"Take your time. I'll try to talk Tiberia down while you're getting ready. Maybe by the time you're out, she and Phoebe will be best friends."

"In your dreams." As she closed her bedroom door, Tess thought how easy it would be to get used to having Zach around.

Despite the sprinkling of snow on the ground, the area around the C & O Canal was filled with bicyclists, joggers and dog walkers of all ages. For Phoebe's sake, Tess and Zach decided to take a more secluded path, closer to the canal and further from the canines. The little pig kept up a brisk trot as they walked quickly behind her.

The pace was getting to be too much for Tess. After ten minutes, she unzipped her jacket to cool herself down. Although the cold breeze off the water felt refreshing, she needed to slow down.

"Is there any way you can get her to ease up a little bit? Phoebe's got to be going at least thirty miles an hour," she panted.

"I only clocked her at twenty-five," Zach laughed. "It's my fault she's going so fast. I told her she could have one of my muffins as soon as we were finished."

"Oh, yeah. That would make me run, too. The other way."

"You won't believe what I brought for your treat," Zach laughed.

Tess started giggling. "If it has molasses and bran, you won't believe what I'll do with it."

"Want to rest for a minute?"

"No, if Phoebe can do this, so can I."

He took her hand. "That's my girl."

His girl. Tess liked the sound of that. She liked the feel of his fingers intertwined with hers. It made her feel comfortable, safe, secure.

They walked in silence until they came to the end of the path.

"You're awfully quiet," Zach observed. "What are you thinking about?"

"You'll laugh if I tell you."

"No, I won't. I promise."

"I was just thinking that it was too bad I couldn't capture this whole morning and turn it into an ice cream flavor. That way, everyone could enjoy it."

"I'm glad everyone isn't here to enjoy it. I don't want to share this morning with anyone but you."

He opened the door to the van and stood to one side as Tess got in. "You did great. See, I knew you could make it. You've got a great pair of—"

"You can just stop right there."

"Lungs. You have a great set of lungs." Zach chuckled. "What did you think I was talking about?"

"Lungs. That's what I thought you meant."

"Don't worry, Tess. I'm not going to attack you. Yet. Just rest for a second. I'll get our breakfast."

Reaching behind the seat, he pulled out a small ice chest. He opened it up and took out two identical brown paper bags.

"Which one is yours?"

"Either one of them."

"They're both the same?"

"Of course. I wouldn't feed you anything that I wouldn't eat myself."

Each bag had tuna salad, a piece of pita bread, some celery sticks, and a pear. "Tuna for breakfast?"

"Sure. The best things are always the unexpected ones."

Phoebe sat in the back of the van, happily munching the fresh fruit Zach had brought for her. The animal made little piggy sounds as she chewed away. The pear was so sweet and juicy Tess felt like making little piggy sounds herself as she bit into it. She giggled at the thought. Zach looked at her quizzically.

"It's that sound," Tess explained.

"What sound?"

"The one Phoebe's making. I didn't think pigs really made it."

"You mean the piggy snurks?"

She laughed as he broke into a perfect imitation.

"How do you do that?"

"Like this." He snurked again.

"Like how?" She laughed so hard she could barely hear him.

"Well, you sort of open your mouth and . . . snurk."

She gave it her best shot, managing only to sound as though she were gargling.

"What was that?" Zach roared with laughter. "You sounded more like a cat trying to bring up a furball."

"Maybe I'll leave all the piggy sounds to you and Phoebe. In my line of work, they would be inappropriate."

"I can't think of any job where they would be appropriate. Unless you were a pig farmer."

"I'm definitely not a pig farmer. But people do tend to make pigs of themselves over our ice cream, if our statistics mean anything."

"You're a number cruncher?" In those bright red sweats and that cute little ponytail she'd pulled her hair into after the excitement in her condo, Tess sure didn't look like any accountant he'd ever met.

"No. You're talking to a woman who's never in her whole life balanced her checkbook. I'm Amanda Rae's official ice cream taster."

"You've got to be kidding. You actually get paid to do that?"

"I get paid very well to do that. But I don't just sit around and taste ice cream all day. Although I do spend a lot of time doing that. I also create flavors."

"Then what you said on our walk makes sense now." Zach could think of all kinds of flavors just looking at her, from her dark caramel hair to her butterscotch eyes to her cherry cordial lips.

"Maybe you've seen the commercials for Teddy Bear Fudge Brownie. That's one of mine. It's already our highest seller."

"You mean it beat out Molasses and Bran Supreme?"

"Yuk. We'd have to pay people to eat that one."

She laughed, and he thought he could listen to that sound forever and never get tired of it.

"Okay. What kind of flavors do you have that you don't have to pay people to eat?"

The sexiest little dimple appeared in her cheek as she proudly began listing her creations from the past year. But Zach lost track—he was too busy wondering if her lips would taste as good as they looked.

No guts, no glory. Closing his eyes in anticipation of ecstasy, he leaned toward her. Gently, he brushed her lips with his, testing the waters.

The waters were tropical, warm, inviting.

He dove in.

Putting his hand behind her head, he felt the feathery, enticing brush of her ponytail against his fingers. Gently, he pulled her toward him.

She gave what sounded to him like a sigh of contentment. He traced the velvety soft outline of her mouth, asking her for permission to enter. She parted her lips. The invitation was too much for someone who'd spent weeks dreaming of his lady in red when he slept and thinking about her the rest of the time.

He leaned forward, pulling her to him, not an easy thing to do in bucket seats with fixed armrests.

She was murmuring his name over and over. "Zach. Zach. Zach!" And her hands felt so good on his chest.

But instead of a welcome mat, Zach felt her lips clamp shut and her body stiffen before she pulled away from him.

"Zach, stop!"

Well, that didn't sound much like an invitation to him. Breathing hard, he slumped back into his seat.

He shouldn't feel so disappointed, he told himself. It was still early. There'd be time later. After all, it was their first kiss.

"I guess it's time to go home." He got out of the van and began putting Phoebe into her carrier.

The silence on the way home was only broken by the delicate rhythm of the pig's snoring.

During the interminable ride home, Tess didn't want to be anywhere near Zach Ferrara, not an easy thing to do when they were sitting side by side in the front seat of his van. She pressed herself so hard against the door that she knew she'd have the imprint of the armrest in her side by the time they got to her condo.

After they rode in silence for several minutes, Zach reached for the radio button on the dashboard. "Okay with you?"

Tess nodded her head. Anything was better than this oppressive and utter stillness. Maybe she could take her mind off this stupid guilt she was feeling for rebuffing him.

She looked over at her traveling companion. The human one. The expression on his face was unreadable, but it sure didn't look guilty. She certainly hadn't done anything to indicate that she was attracted to him. Had she? Well, she'd ogled him that first day, but his back was turned, so there was no way he could know about that.

Maybe when she called him in the middle of the night he thought she was available or something. Maybe he thought she had nothing better to do.

Tess didn't like this attraction to Zach. She had better things to do. She had friends. She had an interesting job. She traveled. She dated, even though the last time had been at Lorraine's New Year's Eve party more than a year ago.

Wait a minute, why should she feel any guilt? He was the one who'd made the unwelcome advance, not her.

Okay. So it wasn't that unwelcome. That was the problem. Maybe she shouldn't have . . .

Zach started whistling along with the cheerful tune on the radio.

Evidently, he wasn't feeling anything at all. No guilt. No remorse. Not even a modicum of embarrassment. Well, she could act just as unaffected as he obviously was.

Tess put her head against the window. The cold glass did nothing to cool her flushed face.

"It's not like I've never been kissed before, you know. That's not why I stopped you . . ."

"Huh?"

She didn't like the sound of his tone. Did he think he was the only man in the world who'd ever tried to kiss her? She'd set him straight.

"I'll have you know that men are always putting moves on me when I travel out-of-town on business."

Zach looked over at her. "What?"

"Men. Men who find me attractive and want to kiss me."

The van swerved.

"Stop looking at me. Pay attention to the road."

Zach gripped the steering wheel with both hands and stared straight ahead.

"That's better. Like I was saying, lots of men find me attractive. Lots. They've kissed me. And enjoyed it. And I kissed them back." There. That ought to show him.

Zach started making choking sounds.

"Are you laughing at me?"

He shook his head, continuing to make the noises in his throat.

"So, men just can't leave you alone. I guess that explains it."

"Explains what?" Now he had her ticked off and confused.

"Why you have to be so careful around us." He pulled over to the curb. "We're here." Grinning broadly, he opened the door and let her out. "Walk you in?"

"No, thanks. The next time you walk up to my place, you'd better have your arms full of food."

Zach watched the sway of her hips as she marched to the entrance of her building. She sure was cute when she was mad. But he'd give anything to know what she was talking about. And who'd been kissing her.

Chapter Eight

"He kissed you? All right! That man looks good, cooks good, and he kisses real good, too, I'll bet." Lorraine threw back her head and let out a hoot.

Tess put down the Aztec design potholder and glared at her friend. "Be quiet, Rainey. Everyone can hear you."

"This is a housewares store. Not a library. As long as we buy something, they don't care how loud we get." Lorraine threw a lime green dishtowel into the shopping cart. "Besides that, if I had a man like your Zach kiss me, I'd be shouting it everywhere. I'd take out an ad. I'd do an infomercial. I'd tattoo 'Zach's Woman' on my—"

"On your what? Concentrate, Rainey. You need to focus on our mission."

As soon as the towel hit the shopping cart, Tess took it out. "Let me get two things straight. First of all we're looking for kitchen linens in jewel tones, not in neons or fluorescents." She waved the towel at her friend. "And secondly—and more importantly, I might add—he's not *my* Zach. I don't have any special feelings for him. Except for his cooking, that is."

Lorraine grabbed the towel in question, putting it back in the cart. "This one's for me. Leave it alone. But I need to ask you something—why are we wasting a perfectly good Saturday evening shopping for dishtowels just so Zach can use them while he's working in your kitchen?"

"They're not for him. *I* need them." Tess reached for a beige towel with a Greek key border.

Lorraine grimaced and shook her head. "Girl, I've known you for ten years, and in all that time, outside of the lab, you've never even made so much as a peanut butter sandwich."

Shrugging, Tess refolded the towel and put it back on the stack where she'd gotten it. "I'm turning over a new leaf."

"Uh-huh."

"Honest." Tess shook her head at a bright floral patterned potholder Lorraine held up.

"That's for me, too." Lorraine threw the potholder into the cart. "If that man was in my kitchen, I'd start spending time there, too. I'd learn to cook. He could set my pot boiling anytime."

"Well, he doesn't affect me like that at all. And I have no desire to learn how to cook. With him or otherwise."

"Uh-huh." Lorraine folded her arms across her chest.

"I don't like any of these colors. Let's see what

they've got down the next aisle." Without waiting for
a response, Tess veered the cart to the left.

"You're sure going through a lot of trouble for
someone you're not interested in."

"Now you've got it."

"Uh-huh."

Whack! The first carton of Olympic Gold Medal
Chocolathon Ice Cream lay split in half lengthwise.
If only she could cut off her feelings for Zach so
easily. "Looks okay," Tess commented to Lorraine,
eager to rip into the next carton.

"Are you sure, Tess? All the chocolate chunks look
like they're on top of the fudge swirl," Lorraine whispered back. "The bottom part doesn't have any
chunks at all."

Tess sighed. "You're right. Uneven distribution.
This batch goes to the food bank. Let's have a look
at the middle of the run."

Lorraine placed a second half gallon of ice cream
in front of Tess, who split that one open, too.

"These are rejects, too. Mark them for the food
bank. Get the production manager in here while I
see if the end of the run's bad, too."

Tess split open the last carton. This one had almost
no chocolate chunks at all. Great. This almost never
happened. Amanda Rae's production team was con-
sidered to be the best in the business.

Luke Reynolds, the perpetually nervous head of production, scurried to her side. "Is there a problem?"

"See for yourself."

"Oh, my, oh, my. I can't ever remember this happening. This entire run is ruined. Ruined."

Tess didn't want to drive the poor man over the edge. "Maybe you should call in a troubleshooter to see what's gone wrong. In the meantime, close down Area Three."

"Close down my production area? You don't have the authority . . ."

All sympathy for the man flew out the window. She stepped toward him. "Close down Area Three. We are not risking another bad run. As Amanda Rae's official taster, I have every authority."

She smiled as he fled the area.

"Well, are you happy with yourself? You've terrified poor Luke. And look at the way you're hacking at that ice cream." Lorraine shook a finger with a long, lacquered nail at Tess. "Don't tell me you're still fried about that kiss thing."

Tess was in no mood to talk about kisses. Even chocolate ones. "Hey, Rainey, are those palm trees that you've got on your nails today? Mr. Larry did an outstanding job this time."

"Don't you go trying to distract me. Yes. They are palm trees. And yes, Mr. Larry outdid himself, and yes, they are quite lovely." Lorraine held up all ten fingers for both of them to admire. "Now that we've cleared that up, you tell me what's eating at you."

Tess shrugged. "I don't know what's eating me. Maybe that's my problem."

"Maybe what you just need is a good . . . you know."

"Nope. No way. I'm too busy to get involved. I don't have time for a relationship. And I refuse to . . . you know . . . until I'm in some kind of long-term relationship. If I have to depend on a . . . you know . . . to be in a good mood, I'd rather be in a lousy one. I've said it before, and I'll say it again—sex is really no big deal."

"No big deal? Honey, I'm not talking about a one-night stand, I'm talking about making love with a sex god."

" 'A sex god'? You think Zach Ferrara is a sex god?"

"Girl, I *know* ultra-sexy when I see it."

"Well, I'm going to leave that area of expertise up to you, because frankly, I'm not interested."

Tess hesitated before opening the door to her apartment. What would she say to Zach? After being badgered by Lorraine off and on all day at work, she realized that she'd overreacted to his kiss. She took a deep breath and unlocked the door.

Stepping inside the condo, she hung her coat on the rack and walked resolutely to the kitchen. Tiberia sat patiently at Zach's feet while he rinsed off some dishes.

"I guess she's forgiven you for bringing a pig into her territory."

Zach turned around. "Yeah. All it took was a couple of kitty treats to get back into her good graces. What's it going to take for me to make peace with you?"

"Well, a couple of kitty treats sure isn't going to cut it, but whatever you're cooking for me right now smells like a good start."

"Then let me dish some of this up for you as fast as I can. Meet you in the dining room?"

"Okay."

Zach was only a minute behind her. "Vegetarian

chili," he told her, watching her reaction as he spooned the spicy mixture into a pottery bowl and sprinkled green onions over the top.

He turned to go back into the kitchen.

It occurred to Tess that she didn't want to be alone. "Wait. Why don't you sit down and keep me company?"

Zach pulled out a chair and straddled it, folding his arms over the back. "I can only stay a few minutes. Phoebe will be wanting her supper."

"We can't have you disappoint Phoebe, especially where food is concerned." Tess chuckled. She took a sip of her herbal ice tea. "I have to know something. Do you put the moves on all of your female clients?"

Zach began to laugh.

Tess didn't understand what was so humorous about her question. "I don't see what's so funny. I'm asking you a serious question. Well, do you?"

Zach scooted the chair closer and rested his chin on his arms. "Tess, usually I don't even see our clients after our initial appointment, let alone cook for them. My assistants handle that."

He was sitting awfully close to her. Despite the heat coming from the chili, Tess swore she could still feel the heat from his body. The unblinking look Zach gave her made her edgy. She cleared her throat, trying not to glance away from his silvery gray stare. "Why me?"

"Because you're a special case."

"And just what makes me so special?"

"Your eating habits. Your food preferences. Your working habits. Your workaholic tendencies. Your inability to cook anything."

"Are you saying I'm odd?"

"No, you're not odd at all. What I'm saying is that you're too familiar."

"Too familiar?"

"You're just like someone I know very well. Someone who ate like you. Worked like you. Only that person didn't pay attention to the warning signs. Until it was too late."

"Your friend died? I'm sorry."

"No, he didn't die. He had to have a quadruple bypass three years ago, right after he turned thirty-five. His job was high-stress, and he had to resign as CEO. He was forced to start his life all over again. But he's grateful as hell he had a life to start over with."

Tess shuddered. Was this going to be a Ghost of Christmas Yet to Come story? "Is this person still alive?" she asked softly. "Is he doing okay?"

"He's doing great. In fact, he's more alive now than he was before the heart attack."

"Do you cook for him?"

"Every day."

"But I thought you said that you didn't cook for anyone but me."

"That's right."

"Wait a minute. Is it . . . no, it can't be. Is it you?" She pointed at him with her spoon.

Zach nodded.

"Wow. You were just like me?"

"No, not exactly. We have some fairly significant differences."

She blushed.

"But you said you couldn't cook."

"Oh, I knew how to light a barbecue grill."

"I've never met a man who couldn't."

"Men like to play with fire."

So do women, she thought. "It's easy to get burned if you're not careful," she whispered, her heart thumping so violently she was sure he could hear it.

Zach lowered his voice, too. "So I understand."

This time, as Zach leaned toward her, Tess found herself hoping that he'd kiss her.

Zach didn't disappoint. This was the kiss of kindred souls. His lips, firm and moist and full of promise, pressed against her own. As their mouths parted, she sighed.

"I think it's time for me to leave now."

Tess sat motionless at the table after he walked away, the chili momentarily forgotten. When she started eating again, all of her thoughts were on Zach, and she could only pick at the delicious soup. Finally, she gave up trying to eat and picked up the bowl.

A note fell from beneath it. Once again, she had to decipher it—she liked it better when he typed. Five minutes later, she finally knew what it said. *You drive me wild. I can't think straight when I'm around you.*

She knew the feeling.

As Zach drove away from Tess's condo, he still had no idea why he'd shared his personal life history with a woman he'd only known such a short time. Of course, he hadn't been this attracted to anyone for years. He'd sown lots of wild oats—and wheat and corn and barley—during his college days. But once he'd begun his fast track to management, all of his time and energy had been funneled into his career. He rarely dated, and really hadn't had any long-term commitments. None of the women he knew had been willing to compete with his real mistress—his work.

But there was something different about his lady in red.

Tess dodged to one side as two teenaged girls dribbled a red, white, and blue basketball straight at her. This whole Sports Megastore thing was making her nervous. Kids of all ages infested every aisle, every one of them trying out new bats, balls, and rollerblades, and not one of them watching where they were going. It was one of the noisiest places she'd ever been in. The entire store smelled like a brand new rubber tire.

Zach didn't seem to be at all affected by the noise, the smell, or the danger. In fact, he'd just picked up an aluminum bat himself and was standing in the middle of the aisle pretending to be Mark McGwire. He looked so cute and determined with his eyes focused on some unseen pitcher and his New York Yankees baseball cap sitting backwards on his head.

Tess walked over to him and held up her hands to block his next swing. "I thought we were here to get my treadmill, slugger."

Letting the bat slip through his hands, he gave her a boyish grin that stretched from ear to ear. "But I haven't struck out."

Putting the bat back in the rack, he stepped closer to her. "You're not even up to the plate yet."

He put his hand on the shelf above her head and gave her a wolfish look. "Oh, I've been to first base . . ."

"Barely," she whispered.

He put his other hand above her head, too, effectively blocking her in. "Barely's all you need, isn't it?"

"Not if you want to hit a home run."

"Maybe I just need to . . . steal a few bases. What do you think?"

Lowering his head, he gave her a kiss that made her head spin faster than one of David Cone's pitches.

He grinned.

Darn that cocky smile of his. It made her want to undress. And she didn't even get naked in front of her cat. "I personally never understood the game. Let's go look at the treadmills." Slipping under his arms, she walked away from the baseball equipment, even though she had absolutely no idea where she was headed. She felt that way a lot these days.

Zach stopped to try out some weights. Setting the medium-sized dumbbell down, he picked up the largest one on display and did a few curls. "Have you been thinking about what kind of treadmill you're going to buy?"

Tess ignored him and his show of strength. "One that works."

"Other than that . . ."

"I checked three different consumer guides, if that's what you mean."

"Oh. Okay."

"So are you almost finished pretending to be Arnold Schwarzenegger? Come on. The store closes at nine."

He put the dumbbell back where he found it and followed her. "And what features are you considering? Which type?"

"I just want one that's as user friendly as possible. Some of them looked like you needed a pilot's license to operate them."

Zach stopped. "Here they are. What's the name of the model you liked best?"

Reaching into her purse, Tess pulled out a piece of paper. She ran her finger down the list of machines. "The Mercury 457." She looked around the sea of treadmills. "It's this one right here."

Zach jumped up on the walking surface of the machine she'd indicated and held up the price tag. "You can afford something better than this, can't you, Tess?"

He hopped off and stepped onto a bigger, more elaborate treadmill. "Something like this one, for example. The 657 model. It's what they have in all the health clubs."

"Money's not an issue here. I don't really care what they have in health clubs, which are evil places anyway, and I don't need all those bells and whistles. I just want a basic machine." She climbed onto the 457 model. It seemed to have all the features a reasonable person would ever need. "This one will do just fine."

Still on the 657, Zach reached into a plastic pocket dangling from the handle and took out a list of the manufacturer's specifications. He held it up while he read it so Tess could see the wonders of this machine for herself. "But look at this. The 657 monitors your pulse, your respiration, and your temperature."

"Nothing like plugging yourself into a machine. I prefer to walk unfettered."

Another treadmill caught his eye. Zach deserted the 657 for a model in the next row. "Oh, wow. Look at this one. They have the new 757 model. I've only seen it in magazines. It has this virtual reality system so you could be walking along the Champs Elysées in Paris or the Nile in Egypt . . ."

"Or on the moon, I suppose."

"Yeah." He sighed. "You've seen it, too, then? This is so cool." He handed her the specification sheet.

"Comes with remote control," she read. "What do you need a remote control for? Wouldn't you turn it on while you're standing on it?"

"Everything's better with a remote control."

"Everything?"

"Everything."

"And you would use the remote to . . ."

"Turn on these base lights or warm it up or turn it off if you've forgotten to."

"Or change the speed on someone who's on it? I don't think so."

"Sooner or later, you've got to throw caution to the wind, Tess." He grinned at her wickedly.

Deep in her heart, she already knew that she had.

Chapter Nine

"We're supposed to be doing this as exercise today. We can come back again and you can stop and look all you want. But right now we're supposed to keep moving. Your treadmill isn't delivered yet, so . . ."

"It's not my fault that the one I liked was on back-order."

Next time she wouldn't bring Mr. Perpetual Motion with her to the Air and Space Museum, Tess thought as she reached out to touch the moon rock. "Just a minute. I've never gotten to touch a piece of the moon before."

"It looks like a plain old rock to me." Zach looked at his watch. "How do you know it's really from the moon?"

Leaving one hand on the rock, Tess took Zach's other hand and placed it on the piece of the moon. "There are some things you just have to take on faith."

He moved his hand over hers. "I should have known that you'd be taken with this rock. After all, you have quite a few of them in your living room. Earth rocks, anyway."

The sudden thrill of Zach's touch as their hands connected overshadowed the excitement of touching a piece of history. She felt like kissing him, right there in the vast, echoing museum, no matter how many ten-year-old boys would be watching.

"Where did you get all of them, anyway?"

Obviously, Zach wasn't as moved by her touch as she was by his. Their timing seemed to be as off as a three dollar watch. Okay, if he wanted to talk, they'd just talk. "Those aren't rocks. They're gemstones and minerals. My Aunt Teddy would roll over in her grave if she heard someone refer to them as 'rocks.'"

"Aunt Teddy?" Zach shoved his hands into his pockets.

Tess tapped the moon rock with her fingernail. "My mother's oldest sister. Aunt Theodora helped raise me. She left me part of her collection when she passed away a couple of years ago. The rest of the collection is in the Smithsonian."

"Tess, your hand is still on the rock."

"I haven't finished touching it yet."

"Well, the line of kids behind us wishes you had."

"My turn, my turn," chanted the little boy closest to her.

Giving him a sheepish grin, Tess reluctantly gave up her place at the moon rock.

"You know, Zach, all of this moon stuff has given me an idea."

"Perhaps a romantic walk with me in the moonlight?"

"No, better than that."

He raised his eyebrow.

"I think I've just gotten an inspiration for a new
flavor."

Grabbing his elbow, she raced down the museum
corridor and out the door. "We have to catch the
next Metro. I need to get somewhere fast."

"Wait a minute. The trains run every five minutes.
Where are we going? What are we doing? What about
our walk?"

"Moonlight Over Maui is more important than a
walk."

"Moonlight over Maui?"

"That's the name of the new flavor. I just now
thought it up. It has a nice ring to it, don't you think?"

"That still doesn't answer my question, Tess. Where
are we going and what are we doing?"

"We're going to a grocery store to get the ingredients to invent a new flavor." She turned around and
looked at him as they headed down the mall. "I'm
so excited! This is going to be really good. It's going
to be better than good. It's going to be an awesome
flavor."

Zach trotted beside her. So this was what Tess
looked like when she got excited. Face flushed. Eyes
sparkling like finely polished gold. This was a lady
with a purpose. Wow, was she ever sexy when she got
an idea! And if he'd known she could move this fast,
they'd be jogging around the museums instead of
walking through them.

"This is too slow," Tess complained, running down the escalator. "I have to get to the grocery store."

"This is the middle of the day. What's the rush?"

"I go to a gourmet grocery for my ingredients. It's down the street from where I work, and it's only open a few hours a day."

Tess leaped onto the subway car a split second after it opened, leaving Zach to board at a more leisurely speed.

"I can't wait. I just can't wait. I need something to write on." Tess looked around the subway car for a piece of paper. Unlike New York subways, the cars were quite clean, but she looked for a throwaway flyer or something. The car was immaculate. Then she spotted an elderly man in the corner. "Excuse me, sir, are you finished with that newspaper?"

As quickly as he nodded, Tess had the paper in hand and was asking a woman in the front row for a pen.

The woman dug through her backpack and pulled out a pencil. "Will this do?"

"This is great. Thanks." Tess tapped her chin with the pencil as she walked back down the aisle to where Zach sat. "Okay. What do I need?" She began writing, all the while mumbling to herself. "Pineapple. I need pineapple. What kind? Fresh? Chunky? Crushed? Candied? Dried?" She listed them all.

"Coconut," she muttered. "Chunks? Flaked? Coconut milk?"

"What are you doing?" Zach asked, looking over her shoulder.

"Don't bother me." She swatted him away. "I'm creating."

"Where was I? Oh yes, almonds. No, make that macadamia nuts. Chopped? Whole? Slivered?"

She knew she was forgetting something. "What else do I need? Zach, what else do I need? This ice cream is going to be a tropical fantasy."

"I think you need less sugar, no macadamias, and no coconut. Especially not coconut milk. It's higher in saturated fat than—"

She raised her eyebrow. "Remind me never to ask you about ice cream again."

"Are you trying to kill the entire population of D.C. or something? Wouldn't a nuclear explosion be faster and more humane?"

Ignoring Zach, Tess began to go over her ingredients list again. "Caramel. That's what missing. A big, thick, gooey ribbon of caramel twisting through the creamy coconut ice cream, caressing the macadamia nuts on its journey to the juicy pineapple."

"This sounds more like sex than dessert. You're starting to get me all excited."

Tess held up her hand. "Hold that thought. I'm creating here. I need to decide whether the ribbon should be more caramel-y or more butterscotch-y."

"No one will be able to tell the difference. They'll be too busy clutching their hearts and falling to the ground."

"I'll know the difference. And if I know the difference, the company knows the difference. They count on me. They didn't insure my taste buds for a million dollars for nothing."

"A million bucks? Are you serious?" Most of the people in the car looked up at Zach from whatever they were doing.

"Sorry," he smiled apologetically at them. "A million bucks?" he repeated in a softer voice. "I had someone with million-dollar taste buds eating my food? How did I measure up?"

"Well . . ."

"Wait a minute. I forgot that you're the same woman who prefers Tasty Taco to *coq au vin.*"

"I'm like a wine taster. Except my taste buds are ice cream specific."

"So you're telling me that you can only pick out good ice cream flavors but not anything else."

"Exactly. You could say I leave my taste buds at work."

"So how do you do it? Just stay at your desk and wait for inspiration to strike?"

"No, I have quotas. I'm expected to come up with two new flavors a month. Usually, I think of more than that. Look, here's our stop."

Running to the front of the car, Tess handed the woman her pencil and bolted for the store.

Tess led the way into Amanda Rae's restricted area. "Normally, we don't allow the public here in this lab, but since it's the weekend, and since you were so sweet about hauling all these groceries around . . . Just don't touch anything."

The only thing Zach wanted to touch was her. She'd almost driven him crazy with her sensual descriptions of ice cream ingredients, and now she was making him insane with her body. The way it moved. He wondered if she even realized her hips were swaying to a rhythm that only she could hear as she mixed and measured her creation. Zach watched as Tess diced the pineapple with the precision of a surgeon, her tongue peeking through the corner of her mouth.

"If anyone asks you what I'm doing, you can't remember anything. Got it?"

Hell, right now he couldn't even remember his own name. The only thing he did know was he had to touch her. Now.

Zach stepped up behind her and slid his arms around her waist. She didn't put the knife through his hand. That was a good sign.

He began nuzzling her neck. She tilted her head as though to make herself more accessible. That was a very good sign.

As his body pressed against hers, Tess gave a shiver. That was an extremely good sign.

But she didn't stop dissecting the pineapple. That wasn't good. Somehow, he had to get her full and complete attention. Gently, he blew into her ear. She shivered again.

Tess scooped up the pineapple chunks with trembling hands and put the fruit in the measuring cup. Wonderful feelings bombarded her, and only a small part was the thrill of invention. Slowly, she turned to face Zach, holding her hands out to the side so the juice from the pineapple didn't drip on him. "My hands are messy."

"Forget about your hands." The kiss Zach gave her was delicious. And endless. His lips pressed harder against hers. They felt firm and warm and inviting.

Tess began to melt faster than a carton of ice cream in the middle of summer. Her bones had the same consistency as the caramel sauce they'd bought less than an hour earlier. She was amazed that her legs were still holding her up.

Her glasses began to fog over. As though reading her mind, Zach slid them off her face. She wasn't sure where he'd put them, and frankly, she didn't care.

Forgetting the juice on her hands, Tess cradled Zach's face and delivered a kiss with so much oomph in it that she felt it, too. Her million dollar taste buds kicked in, and she knew that Zach Ferrara's lips were even better than Amanda Rae's finest ice cream.

She began to shower his face with kisses, the taste of Zach and the taste of the pineapple juice combining to make an intoxicating flavor.

A cool breeze made her skin tingle. When had her blouse come undone? Before she could answer her own question, all rational thought fled as Zach's hands began to explore her body. His fingers left paths of fire everywhere they touched from her neck to the tips of her breasts. His lips began to follow the trail his fingertips had blazed.

She inhaled sharply as his hands began to ease her blouse down her shoulders and his mouth claimed the hollow of her neck.

"You two are melting all the ice cream." Suddenly, they weren't alone.

"Lorraine!" Tess tugged on her blouse and fumbled with the buttons. Zach finished fastening it for her and stepped aside.

"Girl, you are so lucky it's me. Luke Reynolds would be dead on the floor by now if he'd caught you."

"I . . ."

"No need to explain. I'll guard the door while you pull yourselves together."

Zach and Tess exchanged embarrassed looks.

"I'm sorry," Zach apologized softly. "I should have remembered that you work here. I've never done anything like this before. It's just that whenever I'm around you all I can think of is . . . you know."

"Me, too," Tess whispered.

His look of embarrassment was replaced by a grin. "That's good. So what are we going to do about it?"

"Well, whatever we do, we'd better pick a more private place."

"Why don't you continue with your creating? I have some baking that needs to get done. See you tomorrow."

"Okay."

He gave her a brief but tender kiss, and walked toward the door. "It's safe," he told Lorraine as he left. "You can go in now."

Tess was busy scrubbing the melted ice cream from the side of the counter as Lorraine came into the lab, closing the door behind her.

"So is it still no big deal?" Lorraine was grinning ear to ear.

"What?" Tess turned her back to her friend and began scooping up the scattered pineapple chunks.

"Sex."

"Really, Rainey, we weren't having sex. We were just—"

"I could see that you were 'just,' girlfriend."

"No. It wasn't what you think it was. Really."

"Uh-huh." Lorraine picked up a piece of the pineapple and popped it into her mouth.

"I got this idea for a new flavor."

"What, Zacholat Truffle?"

"No. Honest. I had this great idea . . ."

"Look, I don't want to know exactly what went on in here, although I do have a pretty good idea. You were just lucky you weren't busted."

"I don't know what came over me. I've never done anything like that before. Even in college."

Lorraine put her arm around Tess's shoulder and gave it a squeeze. "I'm glad to see you've finally found someone. You deserve a good man. You just need to rethink your choice of rendezvous locations."

"This wasn't a rendezvous, Rainey. You know how I get these ideas for flavors. I thought up a great one. Moonlight Over Maui. And then the pineapple juice and then Zach . . ."

"Sugar bear and I haven't tried pineapple juice yet. Is it good?"

"Yeah. It's the best."

This second appointment with Dr. Andrews was more nerve-racking than the first. The paper-covered vinyl cushion crinkled and scrunched beneath Tess as she squirmed on the examining table. She never understood why doctors didn't give you a real gown instead of a little blue paper bolero jacket and a blue paper sheet no bigger than an undersized towel. She tugged at the stubborn top, trying to close the X-rated gap. "I've been a saint since my appointment six weeks ago."

Then Tess remembered that it had taken her one of those weeks to hook up with Zach, and that week had been a seven-day ice cream and chocolate binge. "Five weeks," she corrected herself. "Five weeks with no sugar and no chocolate, except when I'm tasting ice cream at work. No fried food. No fast food. No butter . . ."

Dr. Andrews pulled the paper gown back open and took the last EKG contact from Tess's chest. "I'm proud of you. Keep up the good work."

Tess clutched the top back together. "You know, Dr. Andrews, there's one thing that I crave every single day but I've given it up."

"And what's that?"

"Ice cream."

"But you just said that you get to taste it every day at work."

"After I taste it, I swish my mouth with water and spit it out. It's not the same thing."

"Go ahead and get dressed, then let's look at your blood work from last week and see how you've done. I'll be back in a couple of minutes."

As soon as the door closed, Tess leaped off the table, ripped the gown from her body, and put on her underwear as quickly as she could. You could never tell when some stranger would come into the wrong room by mistake. Sitting down on a cold plastic chair, she struggled into her trusty miracle pantyhose. Her stomach growled. She hadn't eaten breakfast, because she knew she was going to be weighed this morning. Just as she pulled her dress over her head and wondered what Zach had made her for lunch, Dr. Andrews knocked and stepped into the room.

"You're down four pounds," the doctor announced, flipping through Tess's chart. "That's good."

Four pounds? Tess shoved her left foot into her shoe. Four pounds? Something had to be wrong. She'd been starving herself like Gandhi for five weeks—except for one or two moments of weakness—and she'd only lost four measly pounds? "I was expecting more like forty."

"You really don't have that much to lose. Remember, your weight wasn't our primary concern."

"Maybe it wasn't, but I should get at least some benefit from torturing myself."

"You did. Look at this. Your blood pressure has moved down to the normal range. And without medication. That's terrific." Dr. Andrews ran her finger down the clipboard. "Let's see how your cholesterol's doing. Mmmmm."

"Is that a good 'Mmmmm' or a bad 'Mmmmm?' "

Dr. Andrews smiled. "Neither."

"But it should be a good Mmmmm. I've been working on raising my good cholesterol, just like you told me. I'm walking everywhere. We've walked down to the Jefferson Monument and up the mall to the Capitol, along the canal towpath to the Great Falls . . . and I've seen more weird stuff at the Smithsonian than I ever care to see again."

"We? Well, Ms. Samuels, it sounds as if you've finally gotten yourself a life. Keep up the exercise. Have you ever tried a Stair Master?"

Tess shook her head.

"Well, what floor do you live on?"

Tess looked at Dr. Andrews in horror.

Chapter Ten

Tess couldn't believe that Dr. Andrews had told her to get more exercise, something besides walking. So here she was, huffing and puffing up the twelve flights of stairs to her condo, not taking the elevator—which still probably wouldn't be good enough for Dr. Rambo. Her thighs felt as though they were ready to explode, and her calves were screaming in pain.

Too tired to dig out her keys, she leaned against the door to her condo and put her shoulder on the buzzer, hoping Zach was still there. Just as she was thinking that exercise totally sucked, and if she lived through it, it would be a miracle, Zach opened the door. She fell limply into his arms.

"What's wrong? Are you okay?" The concern in his voice was unmistakable.

"Stairs. Climbed stairs," she panted.

He half-dragged, half-carried her over to the sofa. Tess nodded her thanks.

"Let me get you a glass of water. I'll be right back."

As Zach sprinted to the kitchen, Tess sank into the comforting golden depths of her soft leather couch. Feebly, she tried to undo her coat. Tiberia picked that very moment to greet her by jumping smack dab in the middle of her chest. The twenty pounds of affectionate feline combined with her weakened condition rendered Tess almost helpless.

Luckily, Zach came back with the water just about then. He lifted Tiberia from her comfortable perch, ignoring the cat's meow of protest as he set her on the floor. He started to hand the glass of water to Tess.

"Let me take off my coat first," she said, fumbling with the top button.

"Need help with that?"

Nodding, she leaned her head against the cushion and let her arms fall limply to her sides as Zach gently removed her coat.

Zach set it to one side and once more offered her the water. "Don't drink it too fast," he advised as she proceeded to gulp all of it in a matter of seconds. Taking the empty glass from her, he put it on the coffee table.

"Oh, I hurt," she moaned.

"You shouldn't have guzzled down that water."

"Not that, my leg. My leg's cramping. Ow."

"Where's it cramping? Maybe I can help."

"My calf."

"Which one?"

Her face etched in pain, she pointed to the right one.

Sitting down next to her, he put her leg on his lap.

After he took off Tess's shoe, he placed his hands on her calf and began massaging the knotted muscle. Too bad her legs were encased in those heavy duty pantyhose that had the same feel as Teflon. He wished she were bare-legged. He wished she were bare everything.

Sighing, he kept on massaging. "Better yet?"

"Not yet. Keep going." She closed her eyes.

He dug his thumbs into the muscle, making circles and smiling in satisfaction as the knot released.

"Thank you."

Zach looked at her face, still flushed from exertion. Her hair had come undone. He couldn't understand why she just didn't keep it loose all the time, why she had to keep it pulled back in that bun thing. He drank in the sight of her unrestrained tresses. They were a rich brunette, and when the light hit them just right, which it was now, he could make out the tinges of red that wove in and out of the brown.

Sitting this close to her, he could see her long, thick eyelashes. They formed half-moons on her cheeks as she lay there with her head back against the sofa cushions. He watched as the tip of her tongue wet her ruby lips, trying not to let it turn him on. He failed.

"Okay, you can take your hands off my leg now."

That sure didn't sound like the invitation to passion he'd been waiting for.

"Is something burning?"

Yeah. Him.

Opening her eyes, she leaned forward and sniffed the air.

"Zach, is something burning?"

Reluctantly removing his hands from the most gorgeous set of legs he'd ever seen, he felt a sense of loss as she swung her leg off his lap.

"Zach, is something burning?" she repeated.

Zach sniffed, immediately realizing what was causing the wisps of smoke beginning to come from the kitchen. "I hope you like your zucchini and onions well done . . ."

The Pearl of Calcutta looked as good as it smelled. Tess took in the spicy smells and the many exotic textures and colors surrounding them in the Indian restaurant Zach had selected. Candles in ornate brass holders burned at every table. Large brass vases sitting in every corner held bouquets of richly colored peacock feathers. Jeweled statues of elephants guarded the doors. Gold threads ran through the fabric of their tablecloth, sparkling as they caught the flickering candlelight.

"It's nice of you to treat me to dinner like this." Tess beamed at Zach over the top of her menu.

"I think that's the least I can do after I burned your dinner and stunk up your condo. Maybe it will have aired out by the time we get back there."

"Oh, don't worry about it." She waved her hand dismissively. "I'm having a great time. I've never been to an Indian restaurant before. I know absolutely nothing about this kind of food. Why don't you just order for both of us?"

Zach nodded and smiled at the young waiter standing by the side of the table. "We'll start with *machchi kebab.* Then we'll have some *yakhni pilau* with *tamatar salat* and *khira raita.* Thanks."

"Okay, what are we going to be eating? I didn't recognize a thing you said. I don't think any of those are on the Tasty Taco menu."

"I imagine they aren't." He chuckled. "Let me see. The *machchi kebab* are grilled fish kabobs. The *pilau* is just rice with spices. The *tamatar salat* is tomato salad with mint and onions. And the *khira raita* is cucumbers with yogurt. All of it's delicious, and all of it's good for you."

"And here I thought you were going to let me go a day without yogurt." Tess smiled at him. He sure did look good with his hair down on his shoulders. The glow from the candles reflected its golden highlights. He looked like one of those Renaissance men she'd seen in the Italian paintings at the National Gallery. She could almost hear him playing a romantic ballad on the lute for his lady. Which, of course, would be her.

"You had yogurt for breakfast. Remember? Oh, and I forgot to tell you. Your treadmill came today."

So much for her fantasy. No self-respecting Renaissance lover would even think about talking to his lady love about good nutrition and an exercise machine on a romantic date.

"I didn't eat breakfast." She waited for a reaction. He didn't disappoint her.

"You didn't eat breakfast? Why? You're supposed to eat every meal. It's not good to skip . . ." He was getting agitated. She liked it, but the couple at the next table didn't look as though they appreciated their own romantic meal being interrupted by Zach's sudden outburst.

"Calm down, Zach." Tess patted his hand as she smiled apologetically at the middle-aged couple. "I had to go weigh in at the doctor's this morning, and I didn't want all that yogurt adding extra pounds."

"Eating breakfast won't make that much of a difference on the scales."

"That's just what men think. Women know better."

Zach sighed in what sounded to Tess like exasperation. "So what did the doctor have to say?"

"I lost four pounds." She patted her stomach. "Do I look any better?" she asked, immediately regretting the question. She didn't want to sound vain.

Zach took her hand in his and tenderly kissed it.

The warmth of the kiss traveled up her arm and settled in her heart. Her Renaissance lover was back.

"I think you look perfect, Tess Samuels. You always have."

She closed her eyes, memorizing the moment.

"What did Dr. Andrews say about the important stuff—your blood pressure and your cholesterol?"

So much for getting romantic. She pulled her hand out of his. "My blood pressure's back to normal."

"Great!" He reached for her hand again. Moving it out of range, she picked up her glass of water and took a sip.

"And the cholesterol . . . well, Dr. Andrews says I have to exercise."

"So without any warm-up or working up to it, you decided to climb Mt. Everest."

"I wouldn't exactly call twelve flights of stairs Mt. Everest. But it sure felt like it."

The waiter appeared at their table with a platter of grilled bread things and a bowl of what looked like melted butter. It smelled like heaven.

Zach held up his hand. "No, thank you. No *chapatis.*"

"But I didn't eat any breakfast," Tess protested.

"All right. Leave a *chapati* for each of us, but no *ghee,* please."

"Was that *ghee*? It looked like melted butter."

"That's because it was melted butter. Take a bite—these *chapatis* are just as good without it."

The romance was back as Zach broke off a piece and fed it to her. Memories of when he first fed her his homemade bread filled her mind with exquisite images. The grilled bread was warm and wonderful. Tess sighed. "I could eat a whole platter full of these all by myself."

Zach broke off another piece of *chapati* for her. "So could I." He grinned as he placed it into her open mouth. "That's why I had the waiter only leave two of them."

Her eyes met his. Neither one of them looked away. The piece of bread sat ignored in her mouth as his finger traced the palm of her hand and trailed up her arm in a feather-light touch.

Tess found herself drowning in the liquid silver of his eyes. The urge to touch him in return overwhelmed her. She reached out to caress his face.

Someone coughed. "Here's your tea. Will you be needing any sugar with it?"

Jerking back her hand, Tess silently cursed the waiter, his parents, his children, his ancestors, and his pets. How dare he interrupt one of the most romantic, magical moments of her life? She bit down hard on the piece of *chapati*.

Zach cleared his throat. "No sugar, thank you." As the waiter left, Zach poured Tess a cup of tea. "I believe we were talking about climbing Mt. Everest before we were ... distracted."

Distracted? Maybe it was a good thing. Tess curled her fingers around the warm cup of tea. She'd been ready to jump his bones right here in the middle of a restaurant. First the laboratory at work and now a public eating place. Lord knew what would happen if they ever got anywhere near a bedroom.

"Oh, yes. We were talking, weren't we?" She tried to form a coherent thought, but all she could think about was his touch. "Dr. Rambo ... I mean, Dr. Andrews said I had to start climbing stairs and doing aerobic exercises."

"It's just like anything else." He was giving her that look again. "You need to start slow and work into it."

Tess felt herself growing warm under his gaze. They both knew he was talking about the kind of physical activity meant for two.

"I thought that's what the walking we did was for. Starting slow." The thought occurred to her the walking was starting slow in more ways than one.

"We've only been walking once or twice a week." Zach leaned forward. "That's not enough."

She wondered if 'that's not enough' meant their time together, too. Memories of her ill-fated fling in college began creeping into the recesses of her mind. She leaned back. "Obviously it's not enough. My muscles aren't ready to do anything yet. Anything." She hoped he got the gist of her message.

Obviously not. He was still leaning forward.

"You saw how my leg got all cramped up when I climbed the stairs."

"Maybe you should do something to stretch your muscles. Have you ever thought about trying yoga?"

"Isn't that where they sit around and get their bodies into all those weird positions?" Good grief. Was Zach kinky? She'd heard about people who turned lovemaking into an Olympic level feat.

"Yoga isn't about contortions. Yoga is breathing and stretching and relaxing and meditating. Although I have to admit that some of the positions do look a little odd. I know that it's really helped me."

Helped him do what? "You do yoga? Really? I didn't know that."

"Yes, I do it twice a day. In the morning to get me going and in the evening to relax."

"Do you think I could do it?"

"Anyone can do it."

"Do you have a videotape or something?"

"No. I took classes over at the Y."

They taught yoga at the Y? "Maybe I'll go over and give it a try. After all, it can't be that hard, can it?"

The waiter showed up again, this time with a huge tray of steaming hot dishes, and Tess let her mind wander from where it was heading back to food, where it belonged.

Chapter Eleven

"I can't believe you've talked me into doing this. No cream. No sugar. None of the good stuff." Here it was, Tess's first time in Zach's town house, and it looked as though they were going to spend the entire evening in the kitchen. She would have much preferred to be cuddling with him in front of a warm, romantic fire burning in his big brick fireplace.

"Trust me. There's a market out there for desserts that taste good and are good for you," Zach assured her.

"Right. I'm sure there is, but all the low-fat stuff I've eaten tastes absolutely horrible."

"Thanks." Zach opened the door to his commercial-sized freezer, then closed it. "Before we get started, I have to put Phoebe in her playroom. There'll be no peace if we let her stay in here while we cook."

"Phoebe has a playroom?"

"Yeah, I had this extra room that was basically just

used for storage, and she needed a place to play when it was cold outside, so I turned it into her playroom.''

"This I've gotta see."

The first impression Tess had of Phoebe's room was that she'd stepped inside a giant mousehole. Several boxes of different sizes and shapes filled with shredded newspaper sat around the room. Scattered among the boxes were at least a dozen stuffed animals—all of them pigs. Several photos of Phoebe were on the wall along with posters of Piglet, Porky Pig, and a smirking Miss Piggy in jewels and satin.

Hanging low on the wall, at a pig's eye level, was a laminated photo of an attractive brunette. Tess felt a sudden surge of jealousy. "And who's that?"

"That's Phoebe's mother."

"Phoebe's mother?"

"Remember, I got Phoebe from my assistant, Nan, when Nan's new landlord threatened to kick her out of the building if she didn't get rid of her pig?"

Tess stooped down to get a better look at the picture. "Oh, yeah. Now I remember. Nan's very pretty."

"She's the best darned assistant anyone's ever had. She helped me decorate this playroom, and she comes over to see Phoebe whenever she can."

"Oh?"

"Her boyfriend comes over with her most of the time. He thinks we spoil Phoebe too much."

"I don't think you're spoiling her. Much. Anyway, just promise me not to talk about this around Tiberia. Next thing you know, she'll be wanting a room of her own, too."

"She doesn't need a room. She rules your entire condo."

"You got that right."

"Ready to cook?"

Boy, was she ever.

Twenty minutes later, Tess was still uninspired. This had never happened to her before she met Zach. Usually, ice cream flavors danced around in her head day and night. But who could create a masterpiece looking at a quart of vanilla flavored frozen low-fat yogurt and a bowl of homemade granola? And who could think with Zach leaning on the kitchen counter top looking sexy as hell with his body-molding T-shirt and his snug blue jeans?

"You know, there are other healthful ingredients you can use. You said you liked my granola."

"I do. It's wonderful."

"Okay. What goes with granola?"

"Fruit."

"What kind?"

"Well, I was thinking that strawberries would be good, but they're out of season, and I can't think of anything else that would be as good with the granola."

"I have some strawberries in my freezer." He brushed up against her on his way to get the fruit.

She didn't understand why the warmth of his body made her tingle with this much . . . what? Anticipation? Longing? Desire? She couldn't put her finger on it, but it sure felt good.

Into a glass bowl, she layered a small amount of yogurt, some of Zach's granola, and a few slices of strawberries. "Here, taste this." She scooped up some of the mixture with a spoon and handed it to him.

"This is great."

Tess took a bite of it. "This is boring. I know what it needs, but you wouldn't have any of it around."

"What's that? You might be surprised."

"It needs chocolate yogurt as the base."

Zach went over to his refrigerator. "I don't have chocolate yogurt, but I do have this." He held out a bottle of chocolate syrup.

"Chocolate syrup? You?"

"It's one of my favorite flavors. And I only have it occasionally."

"Occasionally? I thought you'd sworn off the evils of chocolate."

"I can control how much of it I eat."

"Oh?" Taking a frozen strawberry, Tess poured some of the syrup onto it. "Bet you can't just eat one of these." She slid the chocolate-covered berry into his mouth. A drop of the chocolate remained on her finger.

Their eyes met. As if reading her thoughts, he slowly and seductively licked her fingertip.

Tess caught her breath as warmth rushed from her heart to her toes. Her skin prickled, and she knew that there had to be at least a thousand goosebumps on her left arm alone.

She drizzled more chocolate syrup on her now clean finger and smoothed the sweet confection on Zach's lower lip. "It's been so long since I've had any of this." Her mouth covered his hungrily. She tasted the chocolate. She tasted Zach. She tasted his passion.

"My turn," Zach whispered huskily. He reached behind her and picked up the bottle, letting the chocolate syrup trickle down her neck. He followed its sugary trail with his tongue, his lips. He made her senses spin.

Tess shivered and moaned as he reached for the hem of her T-shirt and pulled it over her head, dropping it quickly onto the floor. His lips swept her neck, her shoulders, her chest. "I love how you taste. I love how you smell. Like chocolates and cherries."

One hand found the fastener at the back of her bra while the other pushed away the satiny cups. Her breasts swelled at the urgency of his touches and the bra fell away, unheeded.

"Now you." She scarcely recognized her own voice. It sounded deep, sultry. Bunching his T-shirt in her hands, Tess jerked it off, tossed it aside, and pulled him closer. She began nibbling his neck, enjoying the contrast of his hair-roughened chest against her smooth, bare skin.

Zach pulled her nearer, their hips so close she could feel his body through their jeans. His hardness thrilled her. He gasped as she reached for his zipper. "You're driving me crazy."

Tess smiled, amazed that the sex drive she never knew she had had warmed up, revved, and shifted into high gear. "I haven't even started."

Unzipping his jeans, she pushed the faded denim down to his ankles.

"Hold on. My shoes."

As he untangled his shoes and boxer shorts, she quickly slipped off her own jeans. They stepped together, his hands caressing the curves of her derriere. She had to get closer to him or die. Moaning, she wrapped her legs around him.

He lifted her up and carried her out of the kitchen.

And as he kicked the door to his bedroom open, she knew exactly how Scarlett O'Hara felt at the top of the staircase in *Gone With the Wind*. Ready for anything.

With his first step into the room, Zach tripped, lurched, and almost dropped her.

The down comforter poufed up around her as he settled her onto his king-sized bed.

"What's wrong?"

Zach sat on the edge of the bed. A faint glow from the hallway partially illuminated him, and Tess saw him rubbing his toe.

"Phoebe and her damn toys. I told her not to bring them in here."

"Hey, forget your foot. I know how to make you forget all about your pain."

Taking his hand away from his injury, she pulled him toward her and released his hair from the leather thong that held it back. "Kiss me," she demanded.

"With pleasure."

Loosening her hair from its pins, he let it fall over her breasts like a silken cascade. He sighed, and his warm breath teased her skin.

He showered kisses over her hair. Her temples. Her eyelids. Her cheeks. The tip of her nose. The point of her chin. "You are so lovely," he whispered with such conviction that she had no choice but to believe him. And finally, he crushed his mouth against hers.

She could still smell and taste the chocolate on his lips. With her last coherent thought, that she'd never look at a candy bar the same way again as long as she lived, she surrendered to the passion.

His soft caresses and butterfly kisses became more urgent. His hands brushed her breasts softly, tentatively at first, then more possessively. He explored the soft curves of her waist and her hips.

Desire pulsated the blood through her body as his hands seared a path down her stomach and to her thighs. Once more, she wrapped her legs around him, but this time, they trembled from the emotion that had taken over. She welcomed him into her body, and as they came together, she knew without a doubt that making love with Zach Ferrara was much, much better than chocolate could ever be.

Tess wasn't sure how long she'd slept, but when she woke up, she realized that her arms were empty and she was all alone in the bed. Groggily, she wondered how Zach could make love to her three different times in three totally different ways, and still have the energy to get out of bed.

Just then, he slipped back between the warm flannel sheets and pulled the comforter over them.

"Where were you?"

"Phoebe. I forgot to let her out before her bedtime."

His feet were icy against her calves. She shuddered from the sudden chill.

"Sorry." He moved his feet away.

"So, how's your toe?"

"What toe?"

"I told you I'd make you forget the pain."

"You made me forget a hell of a lot more than that."

She snuggled closer and put her head on his bare

chest. "Do these scars hurt?" she asked, lightly tracing the pale evidence of his heart surgery.

"Only when I laugh."

"Hey, I'm being serious here. Why did you need the bypass?"

"My heart didn't agree with my lifestyle. Which, as you remember, is too close to yours for comfort. I couldn't stand it if you had to go through the same thing I did. Or worse."

"Can I kiss it and make it better?"

"Uh-huh."

Tess looked at the magnificent man beside her. As the first light of morning shone through the window, she outlined the scar again, this time with her lips.

He buried his face in her hair. "You always smell like chocolate-covered cherries, my favorite flavor."

"It's mine, too. There's a little shop in Alexandria that makes the perfume especially for me."

"I hope they never go out of business."

She finished her tender ministrations and lifted her head, smiling wickedly. "Got anything else that hurts?"

Zach raised his eyebrow. He had to admit that the thought of making love to her again was tantalizing, but, at this point, unfortunately, physically impossible. And they had to get to work. Not that he had even a gram of energy left in him. He wondered if their night of passion had exhausted his lady in red, too.

His lady in red. Wow. Tess was so much more than his wildest imagination. And his imagination where she was concerned was pretty wild.

"What time do you have to be at work today?"

She wrinkled her nose. "Same as usual. Eight o'clock."

He looked at the alarm clock on the bedstand. "It's already seven. You're not going to have time to go home and change."

"I'll just keep my lab coat on. No one's going to notice what I'm wearing. Race you to the shower."

"Aren't those the same clothes you were wearing last night when you took off for Zach's place?" Lorraine stepped back from the production counter, tilted her head and critically surveyed Tess.

"No." Trying to ignore her friend, Tess centered all of her attention on the carton of Apple Dumpling Gang Ice Cream one of the line workers had just brought into the quality control area.

"No? Are you sure? That looks like what you had on when we left your condo last night."

Tess opened the lid of the carton. "I have lots of red tops."

"But just one pair of jeans. And when did you start dressing like this for work?"

"It's part of my new image."

"What image? Your I-decided-to-spend-the-night-with-my-honey-and-oops-I-forgot-to-bring-a-change-of-clothes look?"

"Keep your voice down, Lorraine. Someone's going to hear you."

"You did take a change of underwear with you, didn't you?"

Tess whacked the next carton of ice cream in half before answering.

"You don't need to go there, Rainey."

"Okay, okay. Just a suggestion. For next time."

"Next time, *he'll* have to be the one worrying about a change of underwear."

Chapter Twelve

The things she did for love. Tess sat on a cold metal bench in the locker room of the Y. She couldn't believe she'd actually taken Zach's suggestion to come here and exercise. The last time she'd been in a locker room was in ninth grade, and that had been definitely against her wishes. It was amazing the things you promised to do when you were in love. And she was in love. No doubt about it.

To Tess, "exercise" had always been such a dirty word that she felt as though she needed to rinse her mouth out with chocolate syrup every time she said it. But yoga didn't sound too bad, especially the way Zach talked about it in bed. Of course, everything he'd talked about in bed sounded really good.

So she'd just go on in with a positive attitude. Unless they made her twist her legs around her neck like a human pretzel. She knew she wouldn't like that.

It had taken her a full week of constant begging

and bribing to talk Lorraine into taking this yoga class with her. So far, she owed Lorraine a dinner at Rive Gauche, a show at the Kennedy Center, and a day of beauty at the new salon at the Watergate Hotel. This inexpensive yoga class was adding up to big bucks.

Thank goodness the instructor didn't expect them to show up in a leotard and tights. She'd said to dress comfortably and that a T-shirt and leggings would be fine. Tess got up off the bench and began to undress, noticing all the women in their form-fitting sports tops and bike shorts. They weren't wearing enough material to cover her right knee.

Quickly, Tess pulled a one-size-fits-all white T-shirt over her head and squirmed into her black leggings. Good thing Lorraine would be there. At least Tess wouldn't be the only one in the building dressed like this.

When Lorraine dashed into the locker room wearing a big green T-shirt and bicycle shorts, Tess didn't feel so out of place.

"Sorry I'm late," Lorraine panted, "but Mr. Larry screwed up my manicure." She wiggled her fingers in Tess's face. "See what he did?"

Tess squinted at the offending nails. "They look fine to me."

"You need to put your glasses back on, girl. I said to that man, 'Mr. Larry, I'm starting yoga lessons, so I believe I'd like to have them done in an Indian motif today.' And do you know what he did?"

Tess shook her head. "Rainey, I don't have a clue."

"Mr. Larry painted feathers on my nails." Lorraine put her hands on her hips. "Feathers!"

"Did he have any idea what kind of Indian you meant?"

"That man's so dense he didn't even pay attention to the word yoga. It's not like I didn't say it a hundred times, either. I talked about us starting this class all the time he was working on me."

It wasn't hard for Tess to imagine Lorraine chattering to Mr. Larry during the entire beauty treatment. "Couldn't you see what he was doing? Why didn't you stop him after he did the first nail?"

"I had my special silk eye pillow on. Mr. Larry likes to pamper us. Anyway, I take off my eye pillow and I look at my hands. 'Eagle feathers,' he says, proud as if he had good sense."

"What did you do then?"

"I got right up in his face and told him that if he wanted to live to see his next birthday, he'd sure better fix his mess."

"But the yin and yang isn't Indian."

"I know it isn't. That's why next time is free."

"We'd better quit yakking about your nails and get in there."

"It's time. I can already feel the burn." Lorraine whipped off her T-shirt, exposing an emerald green sports top that matched her bicycle shorts exactly. "Let's do it."

"Are there any new students here with us today?" The yoga instructor, a tall, willowy redhead with the face and body of a sixteen-year-old, looked around the room.

Tess raised her hand automatically. She glanced

over at Lorraine, who was concentrating on her fingernails. "Raise your hand," Tess whispered.

"No way. I don't want these people to see that I don't know what I'm doing. They'll just keep waiting for me to make a mistake."

Tess jerked down her arm.

It was too late. The instructor, whose name was Becky, according to the class schedule, zeroed in on her. "Welcome. Here's a packet of yoga information for you. We can discuss it after class. The yoga positions are easy to learn—anyone can do them. Mr. Knowles over there is eighty years old, and sometimes I can't keep up with him. Just go at your own pace, and don't feel as though you have to do everything right the first time." Becky gave her a perky grin.

Tess laid the papers next to her mat. She glanced at the elderly man Becky had pointed out. Mr. Knowles looked like a walking skeleton. A light wind would probably knock him over. If he could do it, so could she, Tess thought. This was going to be a piece of cake. She envisioned herself as Tess Samuels, yoga master, so serene she wouldn't even blink.

"Let's get started. Everyone in the lotus position." Becky turned to Tess. "I'll talk you through the lotus position, but if you can't do it, get into a position you're comfortable with. First, you sit on the floor."

I can do that, Tess said to herself. She sat in the middle of the mat.

"Now bend your right knee and hold your right foot with both hands."

This was a walk in the park. Tess looked up at Becky.

"Good."

"Now, bend your left knee, and put your left foot on top of your right thigh. No—you have to keep both of your knees on the ground."

A burst of pain tore through her thigh as Tess toppled over, accompanied by a loud snicker from her alleged friend.

Becky watched as Tess tried again.

"Okay, I can do this," Tess muttered to herself. "First, the right leg, then the left." She fell over again.

"You need to keep your spine a little straighter."

Gritting her teeth and holding her breath, Tess forced her body into the proper position. She couldn't believe that everyone else in the room found yoga relaxing. To Tess, this was more stressful than presenting a controversial report in front of the management team.

"Good." Becky smiled. "That wasn't so hard now, was it?"

Yeah, not if you're a professional contortionist, Tess thought, visions of being stuck in this position for the rest of her life racing through her mind.

Without waiting for Tess's reply, Becky moved on to her next instruction. "Now that everyone is in their lotus position, let's close our eyes."

Tess couldn't close her eyes—she was still trying to find the center of gravity in her own almost-lotus position. She watched while Becky folded her legs as though they were origami.

"Begin your deep breathing." Becky put her hands on her knees and closed her eyes.

She had to breathe too? Tess panicked, still holding her breath in pain.

"In through your mouth." Becky took a long, exaggerated breath. "Out through your nose."

Finally finding her center of gravity, Tess put her palms flat on the ground for support and began breathing.

"That was good, but it was the opposite of what we need to be doing," Becky whispered to her. "Let's try it together. In through your mouth."

Tess took a deep breath . . . and sputtered.

"It's okay. You can do it. Let's try again." Becky's words of encouragement did nothing to bolster Tess's confidence. Everyone else was breathing like a steam engine, and she couldn't even manage one complete inhale and exhale.

Tess took one cleansing breath and pushed it out her nostrils.

"Good. Again."

Tess took another cleansing breath.

"Okay, now let's start a rhythm that is comfortable for each of you."

Tess took it slow and easy.

"Can you pick up the pace a bit?"

A dozen breaths later, Tess's head was so light it felt as if a helium balloon rested on her shoulders. She began to weave. She looked around the room to see if anyone else needed first aid. Mr. Knowles had a Buddha-like smile on his face. The rest of the people scattered around the room had an air of . . . could it be bliss?

Even Lorraine looked like an ad for the beneficial effects of tranquilizers.

"You've done this before," Tess accused her.

"You're no beginner, Rainey. You're a ringer. That's what you are."

"I just watch a lot of cable TV."

"When this is over, I'm going to kill Zach Ferrara," Tess hissed. "This is his idea of simple exercising? He probably thinks that the decathlon is for kindergartners."

She twisted to look behind her, putting her hands on the floor to keep herself steady.

"Class, now if you'll slowly get out of the lotus position . . ."

Lorraine unfolded her legs and wiggled them. "You're not moving."

"I am," Tess grunted. "I'm trying to move. But I'm stuck."

"Just straighten one leg, and then the other."

"I can't."

"You can't?"

"I'm stuck."

Lorraine put her hands on her hips. "Girl, haven't you ever done any exercise in your life?"

"No. Will you just help me get up here?"

"Here, let me help you," Becky interrupted.

Gently, the instructor took Tess's left calf and foot and slowly straightened her leg. Tess gave a sigh of relief.

She did the same to the right leg.

"Okay, who's ready for their sun salutation?" Becky's cheery voice rang out.

Saluting the sun. She could do that. How hard could it be to salute the sun?

"Why don't you look at the diagram on the fifth

page of your handout to see if you want to do this with us?"

"I'm okay. I'll just follow along."

"You might want to go slow and maybe sit this one out," Lorraine whispered.

"Well, I had a little trouble with that lotus thing, but anyone can salute. Anyone." Confidently, Tess squared back her shoulders.

"Let's face east."

As the class shifted position, Tess found herself in the front row, with no one to imitate. She looked to the side for help. A slender girl who looked like a ballerina stretched her leg in front of her. Her legs seemed to be longer than Tess was tall.

"You all remember the mantra that goes with this? Let's begin."

Keeping her head turned toward the girl next to her as they began, Tess soon learned that saluting the sun was the Far Eastern term for masochism.

Chapter Thirteen

"Great idea, yoga. That's the last time I listen to you, girlfriend." Lorraine fumbled with Tess's key ring. " 'Yoga's relaxing,' you said. 'You're going to have fun,' you said. 'It's an excuse to get yourself a fine new outfit,' you said." Lorraine stopped jiggling the key and turned to face Tess. "You lied."

"Well, you did get a cute little outfit, Rainey. Stop whining and get the damned door open. I'm too weak to stand up much longer."

"Like I'm doing any better." Lorraine aimed the key at the lock. And missed.

"At least you work out. Get the door open."

"Riding a stationary bicycle is not the same as wrapping your knee around your waist while you breathe 'deeply and calmly.' What a crock. Hey, shouldn't you be unlocking your own door?"

"I can't hold the keys, Rainey. My hands are shaking too hard."

"You should have let old Mr. Knowles bring you home. He could have carried you in." Lorraine finally hit the keyhole, and together, they stumbled into Tess's living room. Tess made it as far as the sofa before she crashed, and Lorraine sank down beside her.

Tess leaned her head back on the sofa pillows and stared straight ahead. "I feel like a zombie—I'm never going to exercise again." Tiberia, who had been patrolling the back of the sofa, rubbed against Tess's head. "See, even Ti agrees with me."

"Then I guess that it's a good thing your treadmill's still in its box. Are you ever going to get around to putting it together? There are other uses for it besides just another place to throw your sweater, you know."

"You and Zach must share a brain. He's been on my case since it arrived. But like I told him, I've been busy. That box has only been sitting there for a week, and I hate it already." Tess threw an accent pillow at the offending carton.

"How can you hate it if you can't even see it?"

Tess shrugged. She had to admit that it was a handy place to dump her briefcase, sweater, and newspaper as she came in the door. Besides, the box had become Tiberia's favorite perch.

"Let's forget about the treadmill. We don't need exercise now. We need ice cream. Fast." Lorraine hit the cushion of the sofa to emphasize her point.

Tess nodded. "Give me a second and I'll . . ." She lifted her head an inch off the headrest of the couch. "Wait a minute. I don't have any." Her head plopped back down. "Mr. No-Fat-No-Sugar-No-Fun dumped it all."

"You've got to be kidding. Zach goes through your freezer?"

"He goes through everything. I don't even have a lousy chocolate chip in the house."

"We'll fix that real fast." Lorraine scooted over to the end table and reached for the phone.

"No one delivers ice cream."

"I have my own delivery man." Lorraine punched in a number. "Frank, honey. Tess and I are dead." She shook her head at Tess as she listened to her boyfriend. "No, Frank, nothing's wrong. I'm not headed to the hospital with Tess. I just said we're dead." Lorraine switched the phone to her other ear and pointed to the coffee table. "Oh, sugar bear, you've got to stop taking me so literally. When I say, 'I'm dead,' you know how to fix that ... No, not that."

As her friend broke down in a fit of giggles, Tess reached for the large basket on the coffee table Lorraine had been pointing at. The basket hadn't been there when she left for yoga.

"Maybe later ..." Lorraine promised Frank between giggles. "But the only thing that's going to do anything for us now is Amanda Rae ice cream." Rainey turned to Tess. "What flavor?"

"Just make it something chocolate." Tess hoped that the basket had some candy in it to tide them over until Frank got there. Yoga was supposed to energize her, not suck the life out of her. "Make sure it has lots of nuts. I need protein, too."

"Okay, honey. Chocolate. With lots of nuts. You have fifteen minutes to get here, or we'll have to do something drastic." Rainey made some loud, enthusiastic kissing sounds and hung up the phone. "Who gave you the basket?"

"I don't know. Someone must have brought it while we were in yoga class."

"Someone? Tomorrow's Valentine's Day. And it's wrapped in red cellophane. Let's open it. Is there a card?"

Tess looked underneath the basket. "No card. But it has to be from Zach. Unless my housekeeper's decided that I'm her Valentine."

"My money's on Zach. Open it up. I want to see what's in it."

Carefully, Tess untied the red satin bow. A present from Zach? She hadn't gotten him a Valentine's present, only a card.

"Oooh," the women said in unison as the cellophane fell away from the basket.

Tess reached in and pulled out the large red pillar candle first. "Umm. It smells like chocolate-covered cherries. I'll bet Zach made a special trip to that shop in Alexandria." She held the candle out to her friend. "Here. Smell it."

As Lorraine sniffed the candle, all the while making appreciative murmurs, Tess took out a vial of bath oil.

"Frank and I tried that kind once. It's better with two . . ."

"I'm sure Zach didn't intend it to be used that way."

"Uh-huh."

"Look! Here's a CD of Renaissance lute music. How did he know?"

"Give me Barry White any day over that stuff."

Ignoring her friend, Tess set the CD on the coffee table and took a book out of the basket. Once she saw what it was, she held it to her heart.

"Must be some book."

Tess held it out to Lorraine. "Medieval love songs. Illuminated. This is just perfect. It's the best gift I've ever gotten."

"Looks like he's putting the moves on you."

Tess felt her cheeks grow hot.

"Or maybe he already has."

"Rainey!"

"Girl, I know if my Frank gave me something like this, it would either be to celebrate or to titillate!"

"You're so bad!"

"And proud of it. Let's get to the important stuff. Any chocolate in there?"

"No, but there are some other things stuck down in the tissue." Tess poked around a bit more. "Here's a little bag that says 'Homemade Cat Treats.' Must be for Ti."

"One would hope. What's that at the very bottom?"

"It looks like a red T-shirt." Unfolding the garment, Tess shook it out and held it in front of them. *"Ton amour est plus désirable que chocolat,"* she read.

"What does that say? It sounds sexy."

"French always sounds sexy, Rainey. But this is sexy in English, too. Basically, it means, 'Your love is better than chocolate.' "

"He's got that right."

Groaning, Tess pulled herself to her feet, walked over to her stereo, and put the CD Zach had given her into the player. Returning to the sofa, she plopped back down next to Lorraine. "Cool music, isn't it, Rainey?"

"It's very ... relaxing. What's that title again? I might need to get a copy for Frank."

"If you shut your eyes, you can almost imagine yourself in a villa in Italy. Back when women were women, and men wore tights."

Tess closed her eyes, and Lorraine followed suit. By the third track, they were both asleep.

Tess and Lorraine woke with a start when Frank pounded on the door exactly fifteen minutes later. "Come in, it's not locked," Tess yelled, still unwilling to move from the sofa.

"What do you ladies mean leaving this door wide open?" Frank Davis, a tall, husky man with quarterback shoulders, filled the doorway. "Don't you know that this is Washington, D.C., and not some little hick town in Louisiana?"

"Don't you go knocking my hometown again, Franklin."

His expression softened. "I just don't want anything happening to my honey bear. I couldn't stand it . . ."

"Oh, sugar bear . . ."

"Just hand over that ice cream. You two are making me nauseous." Tess raised herself to a sitting position, amazed at the effort it took. "Help us up, Frank. It's time to chow down."

"You two ladies just stay right where you are. I'll bring you your ice cream."

"And a glass of water," Lorraine called after him.

"Coming right up. Three spoons. Three bowls of ice cream. Three waters."

"What a man," Tess sighed.

"That's my Frank."

"I'm just going to close my eyes again and rest for a minute while he dishes up the ice cream. All that breathing from the diaphragm made me awfully sleepy."

Lorraine leaned back and threw one arm over her eyes. "Amen."

Tess woke up to find a blanket thrown over her and Lorraine and Frank gone. Every part of her body was stiff and sore, even her eyelashes. So much for yoga, she thought. It was just too hard.

She rolled her shoulders and stretched out her arms as she headed toward the kitchen. There, on her countertop by her new cobalt blue canister set, was an enormous bouquet of velvety red roses. No one had ever sent her flowers before. She inhaled their exhilarating fragrance.

He had to have spent a fortune on the flowers— there were so many of them. She stopped to count. Twenty-four. Zach had given her two dozen roses. It made her feel special. It made her feel loved.

First the basket, and now this. She'd heard about people feeling as if they could jump for joy, but she'd never felt that way. Until now. She closed her eyes and could almost feel his skin against hers, hear his whispers of endearment, taste the sweetness of his lips, see the wanting in his eyes.

She opened her eyes. She needed to call him. She had to call him.

As she reached for the wall phone, she noticed that a card sat propped against the crystal vase. With trembling fingers, Tess opened it. In large, carefully formed block letters Zach had printed, *Your love is better than chocolate. I love you. Zach.* And at that point, Tess knew that her heart might burst with love.

Smiling, Tess picked up the receiver and dialed Zach's number.

"Hello?"

Boy, had she fallen hard. Just the sound of his voice made her shiver in anticipation.

"Hello there, yourself. I just thought you'd like to know that I lived through the yoga."

"I knew you would. Didn't you find it relaxing?"

"No, I found it more like boot camp. I can't see why you put yourself through all of that just to relax. I know a better way."

"I'll bet you do."

"No, seriously, if you took a nice, long soak in some bath oil and lit a scented candle, preferably one that smells like chocolate-covered cherries, and put on some calm, soothing lute music and had someone special read love poems to you, you'd relax a lot better."

"No, I wouldn't. That special someone would be joining me in the tub. And we wouldn't be relaxing."

"In the tub?" She hadn't thought of that.

"Definitely." Apparently he had.

"What would you do with the roses?"

"I heard that the petals make a great bed. Soft. Silky. Fragrant."

She knew she was going to have to take a cold shower as soon as she hung up. "You'll be over tomorrow, won't you?"

"You bet I will."

"And I have everything we need to relax . . ."

"Or not . . ."

"Or not."

She wondered if he could tell that she was breathing faster. "See you at supper then?"

"See you at supper. And I have a very nice surprise planned for you."

"I can hardly wait."

Chapter Fourteen

Digging through someone else's garbage on Valentine's Day wasn't Zach's idea of a pleasurable way to spend the holiday, but he had to find the spoon he'd accidentally dropped into the trash along with the empty cat food can. If he hadn't been thinking about Tess and her finer attributes and how he'd show his appreciation for them one by one when she got home, he wouldn't have thrown everything away.

He shoved aside a copy of the *Wall Street Journal,* which was now smeared with fish oil from Tiberia's can of Tuna Temptation. He wrinkled his nose. Who knew what else lurked in the deep, dark recesses of this wastebasket?

Rolling his shirt sleeve above his elbow, he tilted the wastebasket and began to sift through the debris. He grimaced as his fingers hit something wet and sticky. As he pulled his hand out of the trash, he saw the chocolatey syrup which had now worked its way from his fingers to his wrist.

Tess had been cheating. He'd trusted her, and she'd been cheating. Here was the hard evidence, plain as day, sitting right along with the rest of her trash. Zach picked up the soggy ice cream carton. Tess had been sabotaging herself—and his efforts to help her. And here he'd thought they'd been making such great progress.

It was more than just cheating. It was more than just sabotage. Tess had been lying to him. He felt the sharp stab of betrayal, and he didn't like it. As Zach set the carton into the sink, he wondered if Tess had been cheating all along. Other clients had cheated. Lots of them. But this one hurt. This one he took personally.

He heard the sound of a key unlocking the door followed by a cheerful, "Hello! I'm home!"

Zach looked down at Tiberia, who was in the middle of her after-dinner paw washing. "You'd better leave while you can, Ti. This isn't going to be pretty."

On cue, the cat beat a hasty retreat.

"Ti! Where are you going so fast? Aren't you going to stick around and say hi to me?" As the cat flew by her, Tess gave Zach a heart-stopping smile. "At least you're going to greet me properly, aren't you, Zach?" She closed her eyes and puckered up her lips.

Damn. She was carrying a present wrapped in gold paper with little red hearts on it. His name was in big letters on the card taped to the top. She wore that red suit that made him even crazier for her. And she was all set for a kiss. This was going to be even harder than he thought.

"Hello." Zach knew that his clipped tone of voice sounded as contentious as he felt, but he couldn't help it.

Tess opened her eyes and unpuckered her lips, a puzzled look crossing her face. He reached into the sink and pulled out the still dripping carton. "Recognize this?"

Her face turned the same shade of red as her suit. He had to ignore the fact that she looked sexy as hell, and once he got past that, he could do a better job of confronting her. Okay, so he couldn't get past that. He'd have to confront her anyway.

"Do you recognize this?" he repeated.

Stepping forward, she looked him right in the eye. "I believe what you're holding is an empty carton of Amanda Rae ice cream."

She didn't act contrite. In fact, it seemed to Zach that her behavior was more . . . defiant. He was going to keep on asking questions until she confessed to cheating and lying about it. "And do you know where I found it?"

Tess began to tap her fingernails on the counter. "I'm sure you're going to tell me, aren't you?"

He stood his ground. "You bet I am. I found it right here. In your trash can."

Still no confession. No chagrin. No apology. She glared at him, her amber eyes giving off sparks.

"And exactly what were you doing digging through my garbage?"

"Don't try to change the subject, Tess. I wasn't the one doing anything wrong. I just accidentally threw away one of your spoons when I tossed out the empty cat food can."

Tess slapped the present onto the counter and pushed up her glasses on the bridge of her nose as though securing them for battle position. She put her hands on her hips. "Are you sure you weren't checking up on me? How do I know that you're not rummaging through my garbage every day when I'm not here?"

"You have my word." Zach struggled to control the tone of his voice. "Just like I thought I had yours."

Tess didn't respond at first. He could almost envision her armor disappearing as she stared at the ceiling. But when she looked back at him, Zach was surprised. He'd expected embarrassment and remorse. What he got was a challenge. Unabashed hostility.

She narrowed her eyes into cat-like slits. It didn't diminish the intensity of her glare. "I didn't eat it," she snarled.

"What, did Tiberia eat it? Has she become an ice cream taster, too? I hope you're not feeding that poor cat ice cream again."

"I have friends. They ate it."

"They? And just how many is 'they'? You knocked off an entire half gallon."

"I don't have to answer that." Jerking the carton from his hand, Tess threw it at the garbage can. And missed.

He picked it up off the floor and carefully set it in the trash. "But you're the one who brought the friends up in the first place."

"It doesn't matter. It's still none of your business." Picking up the gift from the counter, she tossed that at the trash can, too. "Since you're so fond of digging through the garbage, I believe that's the best place for me to deliver your present."

Turning on her heel, she began to walk away. As she stalked toward the bedroom, she jerked off her earrings and tossed them on the hallway credenza.

He wasn't going to let her get away with walking out in the middle of an argument. After he fished his present out of the trash, he followed her into her bedroom. "My business? You hired me to make this my business."

Violently, she kicked off her shoes. As they thudded against the wall, she unleashed her wrath, and he was the designated target. "You're just afraid that I'll mess up your ninty-five percent success rate. A complaining client is going to be bad for business."

She unwrapped the scarf from her neck, twisting it in her hands as she yanked it off. For a moment he wondered if she was going to use it to strangle him.

"You're not just a client to me." He picked up her shoes and set them neatly on the floor at the foot of the bed next to his gift. "I don't cook for just anyone."

"So you've said." Wadding up the scarf, she threw it on the handlebar of the treadmill, which now sat in the corner of the bedroom. "How'd this thing get in here?"

"Since you kept putting it off, I assembled it for you."

"Apparently another one of my many faults," she agreed dryly.

"You know I didn't mean it that way. Let's get back

to the subject at hand. You didn't have to eat all that ice cream. Don't you know that you don't have to give in to temptation, Tess?"

He could tell by her furious expression that he was digging himself in deeper, but he couldn't stop himself. "Sweetheart, don't you know that I'm here to help you? That you can call me whenever you have a craving for something you shouldn't have?"

"Whenever?" Tess raised her eyebrow.

"Absolutely. I'd do anything for you."

"Anything?" That was good. At least she was listening to him.

Zach nodded.

"Then would you mind bringing me my earrings?"

As he walked down the hall, his gift whizzed past his head just before he heard the slamming of the bedroom door and the loud click of a lock turning.

Even though Zach had prepared another wonderful meal for her, Tess could barely eat it. She put the leftovers, which amounted to most of the meal, into the refrigerator and went into the living room to watch a Cary Grant marathon on the classic movie channel. Now *there* was a gentleman. He'd never dig through a woman's private garbage. He'd never lecture her until she thought her ears would fall off.

But at least Zach knew how to take a hint. She'd heard him leave her condo only moments after she kicked him out of the bedroom. How could he not trust her after what they'd shared with each other? How could he possibly believe that she'd lie to him?

When *Bringing Up Baby* was almost half over and Tess realized that she hadn't laughed once, let alone cracked a smile, she knew she was still seething over the incident with Zach.

Picking up the phone, she dialed Lorraine's number. After several rings, her friend finally answered, breathless.

"Why are you out of breath, Rainey? I'm not interrupting anything, am I?"

"Don't I wish. Honey, if I was up to something, I sure wouldn't be answering my phone. No, I was just coming in from a date with Frank when I heard the phone ring, and I jetted up the stairs so I wouldn't miss the call. What's up?"

Tiberia jumped on Tess's lap. As she stroked the cat's soft, patchwork fur, Tess started her tale of woe. "Zach rifled through my trash and found that carton of ice cream you and Frank ate last night."

"What? Why was he going through your trash?" Lorraine sounded just as incredulous as Tess herself had been hours earlier.

"He claimed that he'd accidentally run across it when he was digging through the garbage looking for a spoon."

"I didn't know you kept your spoons in the trash."

"My point exactly." Tess scratched behind Ti's ears.

"Well, what did he say to you?"

"He said I cheated."

"He said you *what?*" Lorraine shrieked. "Is that man crazy? Why would he go and say a thing like that?"

"Well, he thinks that I ate all that ice cream by myself."

"Didn't you tell him that Frank and I were shoveling it down while you were asleep on the sofa? You didn't even get one bite of Amanda Rae's finest."

"No, I didn't tell him that. He didn't give me the chance."

"Do you want me to send Frank over to have a word with him? He'd straighten him out fast."

Tess laughed. "No, thanks, Rainey. I appreciate the offer. Your Frank looks big and bad enough, but it only takes about five seconds to figure out he's a giant teddy bear. Besides that, I've already handled it."

"And is our friend's body in the trash can with the spoon and the empty carton?"

"Just about. I did kick him out of my bedroom."

"Girl, what was that man doing in your bedroom?"

"Picking up my clothes while I undressed." Tess ran her knuckles across the cat's jaw.

"I can see how that got back at him."

"I showed him."

"Showed him what?"

"The way out. And as far as I'm concerned, he can stay there."

"Uh-huh."

When Tiberia protested and escaped, Tess realized that she'd been holding the cat a little too tightly. "Sorry, baby."

"Is Zach back?"

"No, I was just talking to Ti."

"Uh-huh."

"You know what? I can't let this go. Mr. Zach Ferrara needs to learn a lesson."

"How?"

"How? I don't know yet. I have to think of something really good."

She could almost hear Lorraine smile.

Chapter Fifteen

Tess wasn't going to let Zach get away with his invasion of privacy, especially when it was hers. With vengeance on her mind, Tess stormed into her bedroom and began to plan how she was going to get back at Zach for his heartlessness. And his sneakiness. He didn't have to spy on her. He didn't have to dig through her trash, for goodness sake.

This controlling behavior of his wasn't part of the joyful road to wellness she'd envisioned, and it was about to end, whether he realized it or not.

Shrugging out of her clothes, she slipped into her silk pajamas and climbed into bed. Hugging her tattered childhood teddy bear, she finally thought of the perfect revenge.

Zach had told her to call him anytime she had uncontrollable cravings. All right. She felt one coming on right now. It was a midnight kind of craving. She hoped she'd wake him up, like before.

Zach picked up the phone on the first ring. Darn, so much for that part of her plan. "Tess?"

"How did you know it was me?"

"I just had a feeling you'd be calling tonight. And I have caller ID."

"Did I wake you up?"

"No."

Disappointed because she hadn't awakened him as planned, Tess went right on to step two. "I've picked up a dozen chocolate cream-filled donuts from the all-night bakery, and I'm licking the chocolate from my fingers right now."

"Tess. You should have called."

"I guess I should have phoned you as soon as I got the urge. But you know me. No self-control. None whatsoever."

"I never said that. You backslid once."

"Hmmm. I'm taking a bite of this nice, fried donut." She made exaggerated chewing, smacking, and swallowing sounds into the receiver. "You know, it's funny. This third one goes down as easy as the first two. And I'm not even anywhere near being full yet."

"Tess, please . . ."

"I know, I know. Call you if I get the urge again."

With a smile on her face, Tess hung up, set her alarm, and, hugging the old toy bear—the only male she could trust—snuggled down in her bed.

Three hours later, she dialed Zach again.

"Tess?"

Don't you ever sleep? she wanted to ask him.

"Did you know that Felice's Finest Pizza in the World delivers twenty-four hours a day? This deluxe combo with triple cheese is fabulous. I should feel guilty about eating an entire extra large pizza all by myself, but hey, if I'm able to demolish half a gallon of Amanda Rae ice cream—"

"Tess. That was just one time. Don't do this to yourself. Please. Do you want me to come over?"

"Don't bother. I don't intend to share this mozzarella masterpiece. Good night, Zach." It annoyed her that he still hadn't lost his patience. His voice seemed full of genuine concern, but she was going to ignore that.

Zach sat at the edge of his bed looking into the receiver of the phone. Phoebe ran up and down the hallway, agitated after being stirred from a sound sleep.

This was all Tess's fault. She didn't have to be ruining her health and disturbing his pig, he thought furiously. How could she possibly have any brain cells left after polluting her body with all that junk? And calling him at midnight and in the wee hours of the morning. Didn't the woman ever sleep? How did she get to be a top-level executive with so little self-control?

Wearily, he picked up his pet pig and carried her into the living room. Sitting in his rocking chair, he rocked them both to sleep.

Tess arrived at work exhausted but not defeated from her nocturnal harassment of Zach.

"You look like hell."

"Good morning to you, too, Rainey. I got almost no sleep last night."

"Oh? Did you make up with Zach?"

"Something better."

"Now, what can be better?"

"Revenge. I've begun my retaliation for his lack of trust in me."

After Tess explained how she'd spent the night, Rainey shook her head. "Murder is quicker. And less painful. Come on, production just called. They're ready for us."

As Tess began her first round of taste-testing for the day, inspiration struck. Pulling her cell phone out of the pocket of her lab coat, she dialed Zach's number.

His answering machine picked up the call.

Disappointed, she decided to leave a message anyway. "Good morning, Zach. This is Tess Samuels. I hope you slept well. You know, I've just started my taste-testing, and suddenly, I realize how much I've missed having this wonderful ice cream at home. I'm having such a craving to eat more than just this one bite. In fact, I'm seriously thinking about working my way through the rest of this carton of Chocolate Chips On My Shoulder. Another flavor I created. Have a nice day!"

"Girl, you're evil," Lorraine told Tess as soon as she'd finished the call. "I can't believe how you're playing with that man's mind. You know, it's much more fun to play with his—"

"Oh, no. At this point, playing with his mind is infinitely more satisfying."

* * *

Two hours later, Tess walked down to the employee lounge to buy a bottle of water. As she passed the shining row of vending machines, a thought struck her. She dialed his number again and this time he answered. "Hello, Zach. I was just passing this vending machine full of wonderful, yummy snacks, and I am *so* tempted. You said to call you whenever I felt tempted."

"You did the right thing by calling me, honey. Just keep walking, Tess. It's as simple as that. Just keep walking."

"I can't. It's like my shoes are glued to the floor in front of the vending machine or something."

"Then step out of them and keep walking."

Smiling broadly, Tess slid a five-dollar bill into the change machine and picked up the heaping handful of coins. Stepping up to the nearest vending machine, she inserted them one at a time. She held the phone up to the machine so Zach would hear every click, ding, and beep. Placing the phone near the door of the machine, she crackled each of the ten cellophane bags enthusiastically to enhance the effect.

She put the phone back up to her ear. "Let's see. Where was I? Oh, yes. Zach, I think I have a problem here."

"You sure do. I can be there in fifteen minutes, and we can talk about it."

"Oh, not that kind of problem. I can't decide which one to eat first. What shall it be? A Milky Way? Or a Butterfinger? Or maybe a—"

"Wait. I'll be right there."

"Too late." Grinning, she ended the call and dumped the unopened packages on a nearby counter for other employees to enjoy.

Fifteen minutes later to the second, Tess's secretary buzzed her office. "Zach Ferrara is here to see you. He says it's urgent."

"Send him in, Sandy. I have a few minutes before my next appointment."

Tess crossed her arms over her chest and waited behind her desk for her visitor.

Zach burst into the office. "I'm not too late, am I?"

"Too late for what?"

"Too late to stop you from sabotaging your diet again."

"I didn't sabotage my diet. I supplemented it."

"Supplemented it? With what? The last I heard, vitamins aren't stocked in junk food vending machines."

"Well, I didn't get much out of it . . ."

"Much? I counted twenty-one coins going in."

"Twenty. But what's a quarter's worth of chocolate between friends?"

"Come on, Tess. You're killing yourself here. How can I help you get better if you're wrapping your lips around every Hershey bar from here to Alaska?"

He sounded so sincere, so concerned, that Tess decided to end the charade then and there.

Raising herself on the arms of her chair, she stood and walked toward him.

"You can chill out now, Zach. Stop being such a

control freak. I was just getting back at you for not trusting me. I haven't gone off my diet. Honest."

"But the calls all night?"

"False alarms."

"And your little . . . shopping spree at the vending machine?"

"After I bought the candy bars, I gave them all away."

"So this was all one big let's-get-back-at-Zach thing?"

"You've got it."

"And you've got to get yourself a new chef to torment, lady."

"A new chef to torment? You mean one who can take what he dishes out?"

Zach took a deep breath, inhaling her chocolatey scent. Savoring it. "Oh, it's not just your pathetic attempt at revenge that's tormenting me. It's you."

Before Tess could sputter back a rebuttal, he covered her mouth with his. She was right. He couldn't taste any chocolate on her lips as he explored their velvety texture. As his tongue impatiently parted her mouth, he didn't detect even a granule of sugar. But that chocolate-covered cherry scent was driving him crazy. He deepened his kiss and felt her sway.

Suddenly, both of her hands were on his chest, pushing him away. "Clever way to get your ninty-five percent success rate, huh, Zach?"

"No, you're a write-off, lady. I quit."

He watched as she rubbed her well-kissed lips. And as he left the office the familiar sound of a Tesslaunched object hitting the wall above his head accompanied his exit.

Tess got out of bed after a long, sleepless night. Her improvised revenge had backfired. Zach wasn't supposed to quit. He was supposed to see the error of his ways. The results of his mistrust. He should have been on his knees begging her to forgive him.

Instead, he had quit. And here she was, back to square one. And not just without a chef. Without a lover.

Working on automatic pilot, she headed for the refrigerator. The last of Zach's brown bags sat forlornly on the otherwise empty top shelf. She peeled the happy face sticker from the front of the sack and looked inside.

How was she ever going to eat right again now that Zach was gone? She shook the contents onto the counter. A pint of non-fat milk, a pear, her twice-a-week hard-boiled egg, and a small package of his homemade granola fell out.

Picking up the pad of paper near the phone, she wrote down the items Zach had selected for her breakfast. She looked at the list. Non-fat milk. She was sure she could buy that. She could buy pears, too. The egg was cooked—maybe Lorraine could teach her how to boil an egg. And the granola—whatever she bought wouldn't be as good as Zach's but she was sure she could find a suitable substitute.

Tess felt a glimmer of hope. She could do it. Probably. However, she'd have to have the same breakfast every morning ... just to be safe. After all, before

Zach she used to eat the same thing every morning—a coke and two Danish, one cherry, one cream cheese. She didn't need variety to be satisfied.

Tess cracked the egg on the counter and began to peel it. She didn't need Zach Ferrara. She could do this without him. After all, hadn't she survived the last thirty years without his all-knowing guidance? She'd seen an ad for a personal trainer at the Y. She'd go back there—when the sadistic yoga instructor wasn't on duty, of course—and sign up with him.

And there were plenty of books on nutrition. She could even learn how to cook. She'd watched Zach do it. If he could master the culinary arts—well, then, so could she. There wasn't a thing he did that she couldn't duplicate. Wasn't she the one with the million dollar taste buds?

She finished the egg and reached for the carton of milk. There was a piece of paper stuck to the bottom of it. Her heart began to beat faster, harder. Zach's note. How could she have forgotten about the note? Should she read it? She began to wad it up, then stopped.

It would be the last note she'd ever get from Zach, and she'd saved them all. Sighing, she unfolded the piece of paper. *I think about you all the time. I can't even remember living without you. Love, Zach.*

Dammit, what a time for him to get all mushy on her. She wished she'd never learned how to decipher his writing. Leaning her head against the cool tile of the kitchen wall, Tess Samuels did something she hadn't done since she was a teenager. She burst into tears.

* * *

Zach felt like hell. He'd never lost his temper like he'd done back at Tess's office. Never. What had gone wrong?

She'd accused him of being a control freak. Well, he wasn't. He'd given that up years ago, after his heart attack.

One of the most important life lessons he'd learned was that control is just a myth. All of his employees were allowed to set their own schedules, as long as they could manage their clients and their cooking in that period of time. A control freak wouldn't allow that.

Look at the way he let Phoebe have free run of the house. Would a control freak even own a potbellied pig, especially a pig who had the run of his town house?

How could Tess possibly believe that he thought of her as just a client? If only he could. Life would sure be easier if he did. How could he make her see that she meant more to him than that? Much more. . . .

She'd had her plan for revenge. Well, he'd just have a plan, too. She might be able to live without him. But even though she had a tongue that could strip off wallpaper and a temper to match, he loved her, dammit.

How could he convince her that he did trust her? Did want her back? That he had been as wrong as she had?

The only way he could think of right now to show

her his true feelings for her was mostly R-rated. Which might change to an X-rating with a little luck. But even if he had to resort to some underhanded tricks, he fully intended to win back the heart of his lady in red.

Chapter Sixteen

If Tess ever looked at another egg, it would be too soon. Her kitchen setup made it next to impossible to boil one anyway. And it was harder than she thought. Maybe she should have asked Rainey for help. But no, she had to do it all by herself, and now there was a trail of dried yolk starting on the new saucepan she'd bought the night before and wandering down the front of her stove. A yellow and white rubbery mass clung to the inside of her microwave, and a path of teeny-tiny pieces of eggshell paved the way from the counter to the wastebasket.

Tess took the tenth carton of eggs from the refrigerator. Removing an egg from its comfy cardboard nest, she held it up at eye level. No way was she going to let this little thing get the best of her. She was bigger. She was smarter. And her shell was tougher.

Maybe she just didn't have the right equipment to cook an egg. Maybe she needed another pan—some kind of a special egg pot or something. Another trip to the housewares store was clearly in order. Their efficient sales staff could tell her what to buy. She just hadn't been specific enough her last time there. Setting the egg back in the carton, she returned it to the refrigerator and headed to the bedroom to change out of her egg-stained clothes.

After standing thirty minutes in the cookware department trying to figure out what kind of pan to buy, Tess decided she needed to consult an expert. It took her another fifteen minutes to find someone to help her. The sales clerk she finally spotted looked like a sweet, grandmotherly type. Someone who could prepare a feast for forty without breaking a sweat or losing a fingernail. Tess raced after her as the woman scurried through the store.

"Excuse me. Ma'am, could you please help me?"

The woman kept going.

Doubling her speed, Tess caught up with the sales clerk and tapped her on the shoulder. "Excuse me. I need help."

"Find someone else. My shift is over."

So much for Mrs. Claus, Tess thought grimly.

The second sales clerk she found barely spoke English, but his helpful attitude more than made up for his lack of communication skills.

Tess walked out of the store armed with four pans—an omelette pan, a Dutch oven, a poacher, and a frying pan. One of them had to work.

Once back at her house, she took the Dutch oven out of of its box. She wasn't going to make the same mistakes she'd made earlier in the day, like letting the water boil away until the pan was dry. She'd ruined two eggs that way.

This Dutch oven—and she still didn't understand why it was called that—was plenty deep. It couldn't boil dry in a month of Tuesdays. Confidently, she filled the pan half full of water and put an egg into it. Turning the burner on high, she set the timer for thirty minutes and went back to the bedroom to tackle the treadmill.

She didn't need Zach. Now that she had pots and pans, she could cook anything. And starting immediately, workouts on the treadmill would take the place of her walks with Zach.

If she could find the treadmill.

The dreaded exercise machine had become shrouded in discarded garments. The never-been-walked-on walking surface had come in handy to stack all kinds of things, from reports waiting to be read, to CDs and books. Ti, knowing a good thing when she saw it, had dragged several of her toys over to join the chaotic clutter.

Taking the clothes from the treadmill and throwing them onto her bed, Tess was able to see what they'd hidden. And right there, on the very top of the pile, sat the book of illuminated medieval love songs Zach had given her for Valentine's Day. It seemed as though years had gone by instead of a mere week since their break-up. Taking it from the stack, she sat cross-legged on the floor, and began to read.

The inscription from Zach was printed in careful block letters instead of his usual scrawl. It made her smile. Then she read the words. *Dear Tess, if I were a poet, I would tell you what's in my heart. But I'm not. So read these and know a small part of what I feel for you. I love you. Zach.*

Her smile turned to snuffles faster than she could turn the page and read the lyrics. By the end of the first one, tears ran down Tess's face. By the end of the second, she began serious crying. By the middle of the third, she was sobbing so hard her glasses fogged over.

Tiberia, sensing her distress, nuzzled her knee and meowed.

"Oh, Ti, what have I done?"

Grabbing the cat, Tess buried her face in her soft fur. After only a few seconds, Tiberia, deciding she'd comforted her mistress enough, squirmed out of Tess's arms.

Tess stood up, set the book of poems back on the pile she took it from, and stepped into the bathroom to wash her face with a cool washcloth. As soon as she began dabbing at her red, swollen eyes with the damp cloth, she heard the timer ring. Taking the washcloth with her, and still patting her face with it, she returned to the kitchen.

One look at the stove, and Tess, already emotionally distraught, was weeping again. The water in the Dutch oven had boiled away after all, leaving the egg high and dry. The egg had exploded, and there was all kinds of disgusting white stuff coming out of the cracks. Grabbing one of her new potholders, Tess reached for the pan. Somehow, the cloth was too thin, and she burned her hand.

As she held her hand under running water, Tess wept as she'd never wept before in her life. Nothing was going right. Her relationship with Zach was over. Her kitchen was a disaster, and now she probably had third degree burns on her hands.

Alternating between sobs catching in her throat and hiccups racking her body, her thoughts wandered back to an earlier kitchen mishap when Zach had administered gentle first aid. She knew she should get her mind off of him. She needed to think about other things, like . . . who taught the Easter Bunny to boil eggs?

Tess needed help. Sighing in defeat, she sat down at the counter and drank a diet soda while she pulled herself together. Lorraine and Frank were still on their skiing trip, so she could only think of one other person to call. Taking a deep breath, she dialed the number.

Zach read the same line on the questionnaire Dr. Andrews had just faxed him over and over. He couldn't concentrate on the words long enough to register what he was reading. All he could think about was Tess—the way she wrinkled her nose when she laughed. The way she chipped at her nail polish when she was nervous. The murderous look she gave him the first time he'd tossed out her ice cream.

Yeah, he'd been harder on her than most of his other clients, but he had a personal stake in getting her healthy. And contrary to what she thought, it had nothing to do with his ninty-five percent success rate.

Well, maybe in the beginning. At first, he might have been treating her more like a client than a woman. Perhaps he had been originally fascinated with her case, but now he was only fascinated with her.

He wanted to be with Tess until they both grew old. Until they sat together holding hands in the audience at Georgetown University, watching their grandchildren receive their diplomas. Zach shook his head to clear it. What was he thinking? Here he was planning where his grandchildren were going to attend college, and he'd never even thought about being a father. Man, did he have it bad. And it was all her fault.

There was no way he could work up a profile on Tess, the most difficult client of all. Slamming the questionnaire down in frustration, he got up, shoved his hands in his pockets, and began to roam the office.

"Stop pacing. You're making me nervous." Nan shook her finger at him. "You remind me of a tiger in a cage, but the person you want for a midday snack is just out of paw's reach."

"I do not," he growled.

"See what I mean?"

Zach continued his pacing.

"Look, do you want to talk about it? I'm a great listener." Nan patted the chair by her desk. "Why don't you take a load off and tell me what's wrong?"

Zach was too depressed to fend off Nan's mothering, like he usually did. "It won't help. Nothing will help. I've screwed things up. Big time."

"Did you break your computer again? Our service tech is threatening to triple his charges if you don't start providing a kinder, gentler environment for your PC." Nan's hand was poised over the phone when it rang.

She picked up the receiver. "Hello. Pure Heart Catering, Nan speaking. How can I help you?"

Zach walked over to the fax machine to retrieve another document.

"Of course I won't tell him it's you."

Curious, he went back to Nan's desk. *It's Tess,* Nan scrawled across the back of a memo as he stood there. *Keep quiet,* she added underneath it.

"So you need one of our chefs to come over and help you?" Nan said into the receiver, all the while winking at Zach. "And you don't want Zach to know? No problem. I can keep a secret. Let me see who's available."

Grinning from ear to ear, Nan put Tess's call on hold.

"I think I know how to solve that unsolvable problem you refused to tell me about a couple of minutes ago," Nan chortled. "Are you busy now? Want a temporary job with excellent benefits?"

"I can't go over to Tess's place. She won't let me in."

"I still have that key you turned in." Nan dangled it in the air.

"I don't know . . ."

"She sounded desperate. Something about ruining her kitchen."

"She has a cleaning service. They'll take care of it."

Nan shrugged. "She sounded like she'd been crying."

"Give me the damned key."

With a triumphant smile, Nan tossed the key to

Zach and got back on the line. "We can have someone there within the hour." Giving Zach two thumbs-up and a good-bye nod, Nan added, "You're very welcome, Tess. Anything to help."

Chapter Seventeen

Zach quietly let himself into the condo. He looked around the living room and the dining area. No sign of Tess. No sign of Tiberia, either. That was odd.

The smell of burnt food and overcooked eggs was overwhelming. As he walked into the kitchen the answer to Ti's absence was evident.

Tess's kitchen was coated with eggs of every description—all over the microwave, all over the floor, all over the stove. Eggshells and egg cartons were strewn everywhere. It looked as though her condo had suffered an enemy attack, and the weapon of choice had been eggs. In the middle of the biggest mess he'd ever seen, Tiberia perched on the counter, happily feasting on the rejects.

Tess sat with her head down on the countertop, only a few inches from her cat, surrounded by empty egg cartons and dirty pans. She had apparently fallen asleep after the call. At least it gave him a chance to look at her.

Her beautiful hair had bits and pieces of eggs in it. Her hand was wrapped in gauze. He didn't like the look of that. She looked exhausted. She looked defeated. He knew how that felt.

Making as little noise as possible, he took off his jacket, rolled up his sleeves, and began the Herculean task of scraping dried egg off every surface in the kitchen except the ceiling. He had no doubt that, given enough time, she could have covered that, too.

An hour later, Tess woke up. She rubbed her stiff neck and realized that her burned hand still stung. She yawned once, but in the middle of the second yawn, she saw him. Zach Ferrara stood in her kitchen big as life, and up to his elbows in soapsuds.

"What are you doing here?"

"Nan said you needed help."

"I told Nan I needed help learning how to boil an egg."

"You told Nan that?"

"I sure did."

Her words to the contrary, it felt good to have Zach beside her again. She never knew that a man could look so sexy in soapsuds.

Tiberia, who had been napping by her head, leapt down from the counter and wrapped herself around Zach's ankles.

Traitor, Tess thought. Just like Nan.

"You really asked for someone to show you how to boil an egg?" Zach asked.

"Obviously, it's something I couldn't teach myself.

One more hour of trying, and they'd have to evacuate this building.''

They laughed together for the first time in what felt like forever.

"It's good to see you, Tess. I've missed you so much.''

"I've missed you, too.''

She waited for him to ridicule her about the condition of the kitchen. Instead, his words were soft and conciliatory.

"I'm sorry I dumped on you about that ice cream carton. I should have asked you what really happened.'' He wiped his hands on one of her new towels.

"Yes, you should have. But I shouldn't have called you up at all hours like some kid.''

"No, you shouldn't have.''

Zach gently reached for her injured hand. "What happened?''

"Oh, I burned it on my new Dutch oven. This only proves what I've been saying all along—cooking is hazardous to my health.''

"Do you still want that lesson on eggs?''

"Yes.''

"Let's start at the beginning.'' He stroked the soft skin of her forearms. "First, you need a special kind of egg. Smooth, perfect.''

Shivers ran a relay race up and down her spine.

"Eggs are fragile things, you know,'' he continued. "You have to be very careful with them or they break.''

He wrapped his arms around her as though she were made of eggshells herself.

"Are you trying to say you're sorry?''

"More sorry than you'll ever know. Much more sorry." He kissed the back of her neck.

Tess leaned against the counter for support. It was so good to feel his body and smell his unique scent and hear his seductive voice. She knew without a doubt she was addicted to this man, and she didn't want to fight it.

"I've gone this far, Zach . . ."

And I wish she'd go farther, he thought. Why was she stepping back?

"But there's something I really need to know."

"And that is?"

"How *do* you boil an egg?"

Thinking that there was nothing like a good woman to keep a man's ego in check, Zach began the lesson again.

"Put your egg in the saucepan. This little one is perfect."

"I'll break the egg if I don't add the water first," Tess protested.

"You place it in gently." He smiled at her. "That's good. Now, fill the pan until there's about an inch of water over the top of the egg."

"Are you sure this little pan will work?"

"Positive. Now, turn the stove on medium and set the pan carefully on the burner."

"This is the point where it boils over."

"Not if you watch it. You have to warm it up slowly."

"Right."

"Pretend it's boiling. When it gets to that stage, turn off the burner and set the pan on another burner."

"And turn it on, too?"

"No, leave it cold, and cover the pan with the lid. You did get a lid with this, didn't you?"

Tess nodded.

"Next, you set the timer for about twenty four minutes. And *voilá!* Your egg is done."

"That's all there is?" Tess was incredulous.

"Except for rinsing it in cold water to stop the cooking and peeling it, yes."

"I didn't need the Dutch oven?"

"Only if you're boiling enough eggs for the Washington Redskins. But in the meantime, you've picked out a great set of pans for yourself."

Pulling her back into his arms, he nuzzled her hair. "Even with the kitchen stinking like this, when I kiss you, I can still smell chocolate-covered cherries."

"Your favorite flavor?"

"You bet it is."

"Then I have something you'll really like. I made it especially for you."

Tess left his arms and walked to the refrigerator. She opened the freezer door and pulled out a small sample carton of Amanda Rae ice cream.

"Oh, no. Not again . . ." he moaned.

"This one doesn't go in the trash." She held it out of his reach. "It's special."

"How so?"

She pulled off the lid. "Close your eyes and find out."

"I'm game."

After he complied, Tess found a spoon and scooped out some of the ice cream. "Open wide."

She watched as the full extent of her surprise registered on his taste buds.

"Wow. I've never tasted anything this good. It tastes like frozen—"

"Chocolate-covered cherries," she finished for him. "Now open your eyes and look at the carton."

"My Favorite Flavor," he read. "You created this just for me?"

She nodded.

He took her hands in his. "But we weren't even talking to each other."

"That didn't seem to matter to my brain. All I could think about was you."

"All I could think about was you, my lady in red."

"Lady in red?" She put his hands around her waist.

He drew her closer and nibbled her ear as though it tasted as good as the ice cream. "The first time I saw you, you were wearing that hot red suit of yours. It seems like you're always wearing something red. Even your sexy, lacy underthings . . ." He peeked down her blouse and sighed happily. "I knew it."

"I do have a few other colors."

"All of which I'm dying to see."

"You are so bad."

He grinned as though she had paid him the highest compliment. "What did you first notice about me?"

"Well . . ." Slowly, she ran her hands down his back, inching closer and closer toward his buttocks. "The first thing I noticed about you was your great . . . voice."

"I didn't have much of one."

"On the contrary." She giggled. "It was rough and raspy and dangerous. Like a pirate's."

"A pirate's, huh?"

"Aye, matey." Taking off her glasses, she set them on the counter. "Now can I interest you in a tour of the captain's quarters? Did you know the captain has red satin sheets on the bed today?''

Grabbing his hand, she pulled a very willing Zach down the hallway to her bedroom.

An hour later, in Tess Samuel's kitchen, another pan boiled dry. Another egg exploded. And no one even noticed.

ABOUT THE AUTHORS

Deborah Shelley is the writing team of Deborah Mazoyer and Shelley Mosley. They live in Glendale, Arizona, and have been writing together for six years. Deborah, a building safety manager, has a husband, Brian, and a daughter, Katie, who's eight. Shelley, a library manager, has a husband, David, a twenty-two-year-old son, Andrew, and a nineteen-year-old daughter, Jessica. Both Deborah and Shelley love humor, books, cats, romantic comedies, anything Disney, and, of course, chocolate. This is their third book.

They love to hear from their readers. You can reach them at:

> DeborahShelley@inficad.com
> or
> P.O. Box 673
> Glendale, AZ 85311